THE MUSE ASYLUM

G. P. PUTNAM'S SONS ÷ NEW YORK

THe MUSe ASYLUM

DAVID CZUCHLEWSKI

This is a work of fiction. Names, characters, places, and incidents either are the product of the author's imagination or are used fictitiously, and any resemblance to actual persons, living or dead, business establishments, events, or locales is entirely coincidental.

G. P. Putnam's Sons
Publishers Since 1838
a member of
Penguin Putnam Inc.
375 Hudson Street
New York, NY 10014

Library of Congress Cataloging-in-Publication Data

Czuchlewski, David.
The muse asylum / David Czuchlewski.
p. cm.
ISBN 0-399-14745-4
1. Recluses as authors—Fiction.   2. Novelists—Fiction.
3. Journalists—Fiction.   4. Mental illness—Fiction.
5. New York (N.Y.)—Fiction   I. Title.
PS3553.Z83 M87   2001   00-045798
813'.6—dc21

Printed in the United States of America

1   3   5   7   9   10   8   6   4   2

This book is printed on acid-free paper. ∞

The text of this book is set in Walbaum MT.
Book design by Gretchen Achilles

To Kristina

Yet also there encumbered sleepers groaned,

Too fast in thought or death to be bestirred.

Then, as I probed them, one sprang up, and stared

With piteous recognition in fixed eyes,

Lifting distressful hands, as if to bless.

And by his smile, I knew that sullen hall . . .

—WILFRED OWEN, "Strange Meeting"

THE MUSE ASYLUM

chapter one

In search of an opening for this narrative, a killer anecdote or a quotation pregnant with significance, I have been looking through the notebooks from the months in question. The notebooks, which are battered, weather-beaten and often indecipherable, are filled with the quotes I collected from various interviewees while working, not long out of college, at *The Manhattan Ledger.* I have been flipping through them at random, creating the poetry of a deranged chorus:

since my name has been mentioned as being in CIA in
    newspapers
I can't stop crying, I miss him so much
greater sensitivity to those tangled mental roadways
we dare not allow our society to fragment, among the things
    we have to use

dogsledding to the North Pole in my spare time
I hope to be there when they throw the switch on him
there was a notion it was all of us in it together
this, of course, is the society of total visibility

Everything that follows arose from these cryptic transcripts. The words relating to two stories became more than just words. They were for a time the architecture of my life—a vast system of buttresses to support what rapidly became insupportable. Andrew Wallace, Lara Knowles, Horace Jacob Little . . . they are destined to remain as prominent in my mind as my first assignment at the *Ledger*— a report on a man who walked off a tenement roof, fell seventy feet and survived, bloody and reborn, to describe the way down.

THE *LEDGER* OPERATED from a decrepit building in the garment district. The paper was distributed for free in orange metal boxes ("Ledger—Please Take One!") on street corners all over the borough. It made what little money it did solely through advertising. People considered it an alternative to *New York Press,* which was an alternative to *The Village Voice,* which was itself an alternative to the mainstream dailies. Our readers had to forage pretty far down on the journalistic food chain.

My editor, Joe Fogerty, was an old thoroughbred put out to stud. He had been a star reporter for *The New York Times* in the sixties, focusing on the Vietnam War. He had once been in the vanguard of the New Journalists, the reporters who believed the full story could be told only in nontraditional ways. Since then he had fallen on harder times, trying to write fiction and drinking to excess, finally taking the helm of a marginal paper. He was a bulky man, unable to purge from his body the aftereffects of booze and bad luck. His face was red and puffy. He labored for every breath, and great beads of sweat would roll down his forehead as he did nothing more taxing than make a phone call. Every so often I would catch him looking around the office with a startled gaze, as if surprised where he ended up.

It was Fogerty's tradition to take new staffers out to lunch, which gave him an excuse to drink on the paper's time and tab. One morning about a week after I started at the paper, he invited me to Dignan's, his favorite nearby watering hole.

"Meet me there," he said at eleven o'clock, heading down early.

I walked into Dignan's an hour later. It was dark and loud, and the number of men in white shirtsleeves made lunchtime appear to be a gathering in uniform. The noise reminded me of a high school cafeteria. Words careened from the wood paneling to the black-and-white-tiled floor, punctuated by gruff or derisive laughter. Things seemed to hover on the edge of violence.

Fogerty was at a table by the far wall, nursing a drink.

"This is a Fogerty special." He held up the glass as I took my seat. "Straight whiskey. You want one?"

"Water's fine."

He took a sip and looked around the room.

"So how did you like Princeton?" he asked.

People have all sorts of preconceived notions about Princeton, and I've found it's easier to steer them away from the topic. To praise Princeton is to be an elitist. To not praise it is even worse—you look like both an elitist and an ingrate.

"There are people who like college and there are people who don't," I said. "I liked it."

"I knew a bunch of guys from Princeton when I was at the *Times*. I was a kid from the Bronx with a degree from City. I worked my way up from the bottom. I was amazed by their sense of entitlement and destiny. Sure they were good reporters. They had worked at the *Daily Princetonian*. Only they just waltzed into these jobs. They didn't appreciate anything."

"You reported from Vietnam for the *Times*, right?"

"For a while. It wasn't a good fit. The problem was, the *Times* wanted a dispassionate account of troop movements and casualties and so on. I was over there to report on the *war*. Did Hemingway write about body counts? Did Orwell? What was important was how the war felt to the guys on the ground, not how it might have looked from a satellite in space. I'd send them this brilliant, trenchant piece, and when I got my hands on a copy of the paper I'd see how they butchered it. So I quit."

Another reporter would later give me a different version of events. After a year in Vietnam, during which brilliant, trenchant reporting alternated with boozy dispatches reminiscent of Beat poetry, Fogerty received a cable saying he was free to return to the States to seek other employment. He got work writing more experimental articles for newer, less staid journals and magazines. Fogerty's troubles began when he gave in to his muse and attempted to write fiction. He watched as his more illustrious counterparts—Truman Capote, Tom Wolfe, Norman Mailer—made the connection between reportage and fame. He finally published a crime novel, *Murder on Macdougal*, that received very little attention, favorable or otherwise.

"I have to ask," Fogerty said. "How did you decide to work at the *Ledger*? Unless there's something about you I don't know, you could have gotten a job at *Newsweek* or *The Washington Post*. Don't get me wrong. The *Ledger* is a good paper. Do you know our circulation? Guess. Go on."

"Twenty thousand."

"Higher."

"Forty thousand?"

"You'll never get there. One hundred thousand. Of course, being a freebie helps circulation figures." He paused and looked at the table. "I lost my train of thought. What was my point?"

"I was about to say that I'm not working for *Newsweek* or *The Washington Post* because I don't really know if I want to be a journalist. Writing for the *Ledger* is something I can do while I sort everything out."

I knew people from the *Prince* who went to work writing for the big papers and magazines—people who absolutely lived for the rush that comes from barely made deadlines and late-night editing sessions and catching the typo in the photo caption just as the page is about to be shot. In my junior year, I discovered the truth about newspapers. Words are printed, they become outdated, and you print some more, which subsequently become outdated. So I left the paper.

After graduation, while my friends dispersed in promising trajectories, enrolling in law school or grasping the initial rungs of the corporate ladder, I backpacked around Europe until I became sick of the hostel crowds and the interminable train rides between humid capitals. I went home to Minneapolis and worked as a paralegal for six months, trying to think of what to do with my future. Neither the law nor Minneapolis much interested me.

Fogerty looked behind me, waving at the waiter. I believe he wanted another Fogerty special, although he had not yet finished the one he was holding. Something else arrested his attention. He stared straight ahead for several seconds.

"That man over there, in the blue sweater," Fogerty whispered. "That's Michael Keegan."

"Who?"

"The novelist."

Michael Keegan unfolded a *Daily News* and began to read, drinking his coffee in large gulps. He was a middle-aged man with loose skin under his neck and dark eyebrows that wagged up and down as he read.

Fogerty's eyes darted in excitement. But when he glanced Keegan's way again he abruptly turned silent. He examined his glass, visibly uncomfortable. A few tables away sat a great author, and Fogerty must have been musing that life had not achieved the inverse arrangement, in which an unknown Michael Keegan would gaze with reverence at the successful author J. S. Fogerty. My boss peeked in Keegan's direction like someone trying to size up the new lover of his ex-wife.

"He's overrated," Fogerty said. "In ten years people will be joking about him. His name will be a literary punch line. Have you read anything by him?"

"I took a great class on contemporary American authors. We didn't read any Keegan. We did John Updike, Joyce Carol Oates, Don DeLillo, Horace Jacob Little—"

Fogerty grimaced and leaned back in his seat, as if I had kicked him in the shins.

"Of *course* you have to read Horace Jacob Little, the undisputed master of the postmodern novel," he almost spat. "A reclusive author who lives in complete anonymity. There are no known pictures of him. He's nothing but a voice in the dark. His novels simply appear on earth, spoken by divine lips."

Fogerty frowned and brought his tumbler to the table fast enough that people around us looked up at the noise. There was a vehemence to his sarcasm that seemed out of proportion to the subject, as though Horace Jacob Little had done Fogerty some personal wrong. Horace Jacob Little was a successful and respected author who won, in absentia, prizes and accolades Fogerty would never himself receive. It must have offended him that an author blessed with such prodigious gifts refused to unmask himself to his votaries.

"You agree he's a great writer, don't you?" I asked.

"Sure. A great writer. And a coward. I mean, who does he think he is? Imagine an author too good to sign his own books or grant interviews. Like he's goddamn Homer or something."

"He used to be my favorite writer. I guess he still is."

A new look had come into Fogerty's eyes, replacing the fog of alcohol and jealousy. His mien was clear, intense. "What if we tried to find him?" he said. "I've always dreamed of nailing the bastard and putting his picture on the front page."

"I really don't think it's possible."

"Why not? He's a person just like everyone else. I refuse to believe that someone could live nowadays without leaving any trace of having existed."

"But he's been anonymous for twenty-five years. He must have found ways of avoiding all the obvious pitfalls. Anyway, doesn't the guy deserve his privacy? What would give us the right to expose him?"

"When he writes a book, he puts himself forward as an authority. He's *more* than a celebrity, not less. He's trying to tell us things about life. He can't do that and expect us to let him turn around and hide. He's already given up his right to privacy by writing."

"I don't think it can be done," I said. Still, I had wondered about Horace Jacob Little's identity since I first read him in high school. I didn't agree with Fogerty's analysis of his rights, but the idea of finding Horace Jacob Little intrigued me. It might be possible to interview him and let him return to his reclusive life-style having gone, for once, on the record. Maybe he was even waiting for someone to find him.

Fogerty slapped the table and smiled. "This is your long-term assignment. You still write the weekly pieces I give you. But I want you to keep working on Horace Jacob Little. If you're meant to be a reporter, this is a story you can really sink your teeth into."

He went to the bar for another drink. Passing Michael Keegan, he craned his neck to see what the author was reading. Keegan looked up as if to say, *Do you mind?* Fogerty nodded and moved on.

I realized Fogerty was not going to order any food during our lunch, so I turned around to look for the waiter. The voluble atmosphere of the bar had changed into something more sinister. The men in shirtsleeves were hunched over their tables, eyeing each other and whispering suggestively. I imagined for a moment that I was entangled in the highest levels of the intelligence community. The air was alive with secrets. And any person, other than me, could have been Horace Jacob Little.

CHaPTer TWO

I have no memory of the days I first learned about music, language or the sea. But I remember discovering Horace Jacob Little.

A stray paperback, overstocked or misordered, fell into the possession of my high school English teacher. Recognizing nothing of what would come of it, she gave me this copy of *The Unreal City,* Horace Jacob Little's early masterpiece of love and betrayal. It did not look promising to me. Of the book's six hundred pages, the first twenty provided a detailed history and geography of its fictional setting. At the time I was a fan of books in which vampires have killed several people by page twenty. Worst of all, the cover was blank except for the title and the author's name. It looked unfinished— something long and tedious that the publisher simply gave up on and sent out without bothering to commission artwork.

I let the book sit around before boredom drove me to pick it up on an idle weekend. I read it straight through, over the course of twenty-three exhausting hours. Never before had a novel burdened me with the anxiety of participating in a tragedy. The death scene in the final chapter struck me with the force of revelation. As I read the last paragraph, I cried silently—whether from sadness or exhilaration, I did not know. I had stumbled unprepared into a more troubling understanding of the world. The pain and doubt that ran throughout *The Unreal City* were promises of what I would find in my own future, but the prose was so beautiful and the story so fascinating that I was grateful for the appalling knowledge. Horace Jacob Little's book was an incantation that dispelled the calm certainties of my childhood.

I soon made my way through every Horace Jacob Little book. His work staked out for itself a corner in my consciousness. I inscribed my name carefully on the inside of the covers: JAKE BURNETT. My world took on shades of Horace Jacob Little's fictions. I adored him with the reverence for a writer that only a high school senior could muster.

My own enthusiasm aside, Horace Jacob Little was more talked about than read. He was most famous for the strange circumstances of his personality, for his seclusion, his solitude. He was not much more than a fiction himself. His true identity was a mystery. Legend had it that not even his agent had met him, that they communicated via post office box. Horace Jacob Little had insisted on blank covers for all his books. No illustrations, no capsule biographies, no author photographs, no laudatory blurbs. He had never granted an interview. No one knew what he looked like or where he lived. He was less a person than an anonymous evangelist, holed up somewhere, writing words as a greater spirit moved him. I used to imagine him: a death row inmate, a mild-mannered accountant, a disfigured cripple . . .

He was none of these, as it turned out, nothing my imagination could conjure.

IN CONTRAST TO his first books, Horace Jacob Little's later work was experimental and difficult, filled with allusions and bursts of madcap, sometimes barely intelligible prose. Many people preferred the later books, such as *Strange Meeting*, which were certainly more celebrated. To me, however, his best work was his earliest. Take, for instance, the title story from his 1974 collection, *The Length of New Jersey*.

A man on a train is startled from a daydream by a pat on the head. A mother and her young child are sitting behind him, and the man has been listening to her narrate the journey to the child: "Look at the river and all the ice." "Look at the girl playing basketball—do you see the girl?" To all these questions the child responds with preverbal noise, seemingly on the verge of recognizable words. The pat on the man's head draws a gentle rebuke from the mother: "Don't hit the man on the head, that's not nice." The man half turns and smiles at the mother to let her know he is not offended.

As the trip goes on, the mother continues to point out the world to her child. The man becomes enraptured by the mother's loving tone and the squeals of delight from the boy. Eventually the man asks the age of the child, hoping to make conversation on what would be an agreeable topic. The mother smiles broadly and says, "Five. He hasn't learned to talk yet, but he's trying." The man turns fully around to observe the child for the first time and realizes that the boy is not as young as he thought. He is developmentally disabled. The man sinks into a silent depression, and as the train rolls into the dusky industrial landscape around Hoboken, the world seems to him a blighted place, where beauty gives way to deformity.

When the train reaches the Hoboken terminus, the man rises and removes his suitcase from the overhead rack. The mother says to her child, "Look at the man's great big suitcase. He must have been traveling for real, not just for fun." The man takes this to mean that the trip has been entertainment for the boy. When he looks again at the pair he understands that the mother would do anything for her child, even take him on a two-hour train ride for fun. The grimy factory landscape is beautiful and endlessly engrossing to the child. The disease the man had callously considered a catastrophe is immaterial to the radiant mother.

The last paragraph:

"He lost them in the crowd, mother and child. With a surge of anxiety and disappointment he realized that the journey was indeed over. He began a solitary walk through the deathly silent streets. As he passed from the brightness of the station into the shadows, he wished the train could have continued all night and forever, down the entire length of New Jersey."

Whenever I finished a story or a novel by Horace Jacob Little, regardless of its vintage, I felt my horizons expanding, his words allowing me to live in newly liberated territory. I even suspected that his stories were answers to questions just beyond formulation, clues to why I was alive in the first place.

NO MATTER WHAT I thought of Horace Jacob Little's fiction, it was an incident during a morning lecture at Princeton that cemented his hold on my imagination. The lecture hall was full of students drinking coffee, whispering to one another the happenings of the night before. Professor Mullin, with his owl glasses and rumpled hair, his chalk-stained tweed blazer and wool tie, blew into his clip-on microphone to quiet the crowd.

"We consider today one of the most fascinating enigmas of twentieth-century literature," he said, pacing the stage. He often spoke in qualified superlatives. "A man with no history, a text with no source. The almost perfect corollary, if you will, of an age of absurdity and dislocation."

He reviewed what little was known of the historical Horace Jacob Little. He had grown up on Long Island, the son of a machinist and a homemaker. He published his first novel at twenty-five, soon after graduating from Brown. He lived for a time in Mexico, then Vienna. He underwent a literary transformation in mid-career, from realistic novels like *The Unreal City* to metaphysical stories like those in *Strange Meeting*. Mullin discussed several aspects of individual stories in *Strange Meeting*: the title story, in which a mysterious doppelgänger abducts a scholar obsessed with Dante's *Inferno*; "The Lord of Close Vicinity," a meditation on the return of Columbus to the Old World; "The History of London," in which someone tries to record everything that happened in a single day in that city.

"I personally prefer his later work," Mullin said, pacing faster, the movement of his legs seeming to propel his thoughts. "The early novels are overwrought and to my ears pretentious. Many would disagree and call his later work contrived and soulless. With Horace Jacob Little, the main point is that we are limited to what we can glean from these works alone. We cannot ask him for help or guidance."

I noticed a man inching up the side aisle, hunched over and grasping at the wall. He was dressed in a heavy overcoat and a winter hat, even though it was a spring day. His face was grizzled and dirty. I could hear him mumbling to himself as he passed me. Mullin saw the man but continued to lecture.

Once the man had made his way up the aisle, he climbed onto the stage. All eyes in the lecture hall were on him. Mullin, taken aback, asked if he needed help.

"I'd like to say a few words to the class if it's okay with you, man."

He put his right hand in his coat pocket and pointed it at Mullin, as if holding a weapon. Mullin moved away from the lectern.

The man cleared his throat and began to speak. He announced that the government was after him. He said the United Nations had implanted sensors in his brain. He told us he had been visited by space aliens.

He also identified himself as Horace Jacob Little.

After a few minutes campus police flooded the room and tackled the man. They removed him, screaming and cursing, from the lecture hall.

Mullin returned to the lectern and spoke over the excited buzzing of the students.

"The amazing thing is that no one can prove that was *not* Horace Jacob Little," he said. "Maybe that was some wacko. Maybe it was the author himself, acting crazy for reasons known only to him. Or maybe it was an actor I hired to illustrate a point about anonymity and its consequences. In the end, we'll never know."

I DID NOT see him at the time, but I have often imagined my classmate Andrew Wallace sitting in the back of the lecture hall, watching this spectacle. Andrew's life would never be the same. Something inside his mind struck a note and completed a harmony he had been composing over several confused months. In that moment a new world took shape in his mind. His thoughts accelerated to an unprecedented and dangerous speed. He was startled and hyperalert, as when we see an unexpected movement in the dark. *If this isn't Horace Jacob Little*, he thought, *then who is? Who is?*

But I did not see him. I missed the moment when the general terrain of his life, and mine, was established. I would later read Andrew's account of all this in his *Confessions*, the document he wrote at Overlook Psychiatric Institute in which he purports to reveal the secret of Horace Jacob Little's identity.

IT WAS DURING freshman year that I made my first abortive attempt to locate Horace Jacob Little. I had just finished rereading *Strange Meeting*, and I found my roommate, George Faber, sitting at his computer playing Martian Slaughter.

The computer had always been the most important thing in George's life. He would play gory death games like Martian Slaughter for hours and hours, finally yelling at four in the morning that he had won—he had beaten back the starcruiser of the Galactic Empire and saved a grateful humankind. In his serious moments he wrote computer programs with what I was told was the genius of an artist. His expensive machine, which he designed and assembled himself from an assortment of green circuit boards, stayed on continuously, whirring and chirping. He believed it was too damaging to turn it on and off.

"Check it out," he said. "I'm in level seven, the subterranean headquarters of the Galactic Overlords."

I watched him maneuver through the two-dimensional world, the mouse moving fitfully. Misshapen aliens came from the shadows, foaming at the mouth. George peppered them with orange rays. The speakers screeched with their death cries. Two aliens managed to gang up on him, and he could kill only one before the other closed in, chomping away with its razor-studded mouth.

"Shit," George said, slapping the computer monitor on its side. Blood flowed down the screen.

"Let me ask you something," I said. "If I wanted to use your computer to find someone who doesn't want to be found, what would I do?"

"Who are you looking for?"

"Horace Jacob Little."

George pitched his chair back and put his feet on the desk next to the computer.

"It would take some effort. You would have to hack into something like the Department of Motor Vehicles or the IRS."

"You could do that, right?"

He shrugged, too modest or careful to admit the extent of his talents. "You don't even know if that's his real name, do you?"

"No. I guess it could be a pseudonym."

"Are you sure he's in this country?"

"No."

"Are you even sure he exists?"

"What do you mean?"

"Maybe if you hired a person full-time to search all the databases of the world, you might find something. But probably not. Anyway, even if you found Horace Jacob Little, what would you do about it?"

I was considering my answer when Lara Knowles entered our room without knocking. She lived down the hall in our dorm, which was informally known as the Monastery. Even after the arrival of coeducation, those dozen rooms in Blair East—a modest extension off the more majestic Blair Hall—had remained open only to men. This was the Monastery, and there was an analogous Nunnery across the quad. Before I showed up they repealed the rules. Nuns moved in with monks and vice versa.

"Let's get dinner," she said to me. We ate together almost every night. At that point in the year I spent much of my time plotting strategies to move our relationship beyond this state of friendship. George usually joined us at dinner, along with a bunch of other monks and nuns, but I paid almost all my attention to Lara. I was thrilled when she reciprocated.

I grabbed a coat. George said, "Is it stuffed shells tonight?" I walked in the cool night next to Lara, weighing the consequences of putting my hand on her back.

All thoughts of Horace Jacob Little were forgotten.

cнартеr тнree

This is an account of what I have done on earth and the condition of the place as I found it.

I will immediately make my central accusation, striking for the first time my unfortunate theme. Horace Jacob Little is engaged in a secret campaign against me. I do not know the exact reason for this. The existence of a worldwide cabal with the power to control events and manipulate destiny is almost too awful to imagine, but I have seen the evidence and will present it accordingly.

I am keeping in mind that this document may well play a central role in a future trial. The circumstances of its composition are not immaterial. I am being held here at the Overlook hospital, not entirely against my will. They are encouraging me to write this report. They have given me a box of felt-tipped pens and reams of blank paper intended for use in a Xerox machine. My suspicion is that they are acting on the orders of Horace Jacob Little. He wants to discover how much I know. He has followed me, tormented me, attempted to direct my life according to the obscure logic of his unrevealed desires. For the record, I can forgive much of this. He is a great man. If he sees fit to concern himself with me, who am I to question his reasons?

Lara, my love, if only Horace Jacob Little hadn't identified you. If only he could have left you alone. He saw our perfect happiness and couldn't resist destroying it. It was an act of gratuitous evil and it reveals the utter emptiness of his heart. No one has more absolute power, more silent authority over events, than Horace Jacob Little. For this, Lara, for you, for us, I have decided to take revenge when the opportunity presents itself. Dr. Saunders is eager to hear about this plan. He is working for Horace Jacob Little and has been charged with protecting him from me.

—Tell me more about your wish to attack Horace Jacob Little, he says, folding his hands over his stomach.

I smile and change the subject.

I WAS BORN in 1978, at the hospital of Ramstein Air Force Base in Germany. Kaiserslautern was the first of a long succession of nomadic hometowns, as my mother and I followed my father from base to base. I stayed put for three years in Ohio, between the ages of six and nine. Those are the years for which I remember the names and faces of my classmates and schoolteachers. The details of other early places and people are too hazy to recall in definite terms. I spent much of my time at home, and my mother took the opportunity to teach me. In fact, I was absent so much that I was largely home-schooled.

In retrospect, I can see there were countless souls struggling to control my actions. I call this the Darwinism of Souls. At birth, we are fitted with a multitude of souls. As we grow, those souls that are unfit shrivel and die, as a result of the circumstances in which the body finds itself. Finally one soul wins and defines the personality. How often have we thought it is as if different souls inhabited the same child, so changeable were its actions and thoughts? In the physiological world, the Darwinian process leads to the formation of wonderful and complex phenomena such as the eye. In the psychological world, this process leads to the formation of an object no less phenomenal— the individual.

I have written a small monograph on this subject. Horace Jacob Little has prevented me from publishing it. He will no doubt squelch the present text as well—too close to the truth, too real, too revelatory. On the bright side, this gives me the freedom to write what I want, since no one will ever read it, and the words become like water in water as they leave my pen.

HERE IS AS good a place as any to address the matter of my present state of mind. Dr. Saunders suggests all is not well with my conception of reality. The truth is that I have never felt more certain of the actual nature of things. My experiences with Horace Jacob Little have been a great revelation. I have stolen a glimpse under the door that imprisons me, imprisons us all. That I am attempting to convince a skeptical reader via a communiqué from a mental facility is inconvenient, but unavoidable. The reader will soon see that this report is the product of a mind filled with a burdensome secret, not with snakes and recurring staircases.

BACK IN OHIO, there was a girl named Laura who would spend time with me. I remember her backyard in great detail. The grass was always burnt tan, rather than green. An old swing set stood in the middle of the yard. It had once been painted white with red and blue stripes, but this design was faded and obscured by roseolas of rust. Toward the back line of scrub trees was a small cemetery for pets, complete with headstones and flowers. We were not allowed to play near the pets.

My happiest moments were in her den playing ColecoVision or running through her backyard after wading in her kiddy pool. In college, I found my true love, whose name is Lara.

If I believed in coincidence, the resemblance between the names would be remarkable.

I was an awkward child. Whom do I blame for this? Perhaps my teachers, who were eager to quash my natural curiosity, or my peers, who knew I was different even before I did. I skipped several grades in school, since whenever we moved I would start in a new class without friends anyway. I was usually the smallest in the class.

I was obsessive about homework, often rereading the same chapter twenty times before a test. At that level of concentration I could quote entire passages from memory. I had a vocabulary and a facility with language well beyond my years, and an innate eye for patterns below the surface of events. I enjoyed the order of math problems, and would often calculate complicated sums and perform complex operations in my head as I fell asleep.

I was always first in the class. I was so lonely I would have given it all away for only one true friend.

I felt different from other kids even in my relationship to my parents. Other parents were tied down to specific houses, and their love for their children seemed part and parcel of that attachment to place. I never felt that anywhere I lived was truly home. My parents were at each place, of course, but even they seemed somewhat bewildered by the new surroundings.

———————

EVEN AS I write this, they are using upon me an old torture devised by the Borgias. You arrest a man and put him not in prison, but in a well-furnished apartment with good books, fine wine and gourmet food. The man thinks to himself: Well, this isn't so bad at all. After a few days it seems that the room is smaller. It must be his imagination. He's only getting used to the place. A few days later, the conviction is stronger. Still he dismisses it. Finally it becomes clear. He is going to be crushed to death by the slowly closing walls. The realization always makes the prisoner lose his mind.

That is what they are doing to me. I can sense them moving. I hear it in the quiet of the night. They are measuring off in inches the balance of my allotted time.

I HAVE SKETCHED the rudiments of an unhappy, or perhaps only intermittently happy, youth. There remains nothing of relevance to be told about those years, since the person I am now was not then in control of my body. The soul that has survived the Darwinian winnowing and that now directs my life was only along for the ride on those early adventures, biding its time, waiting for the proper moment to wrest control from its weaker antecedents. I carry with me the memory of my childhood, but it is only a blurred memory, the tracings on my present soul of the workings and errors of its predecessors.

I can date the precise moment of this changeover. Shortly before I went off to college at Princeton, I became extremely sick. My temperature went as high as 105 degrees Fahrenheit. I hallucinated wildly. I traveled in a time machine back to the age of the dinosaurs and was left to my own devices among towering tyrannosaurs and deceptively docile smaller beasts. I wandered throughout the cities and countries of the world, aware that I was the only person left on earth. I floated down endless rivers shrouded in fog and overgrown with dark foliage. I disembarked and bushwhacked with bands of natives, finding strange animals and villages where Dionysiac celebrations shook the earth. I flew on a spaceship into the sun across the chaos of nothingness, hotter and hotter and hotter until nothing was left but my thoughts. During this delirium, this impromptu Vision Quest, the soul of my childhood was vanquished. When I woke, my introversion gradually disappeared. I no longer felt limited to the confines of books and imaginary numbers. I wanted to explore the world, talking to everyone I found. Life as an adult beckoned with the promise of a new start, which I now understand was the promise of a new soul.

My reader has presumably noticed that no one remembers very much from childhood. This points to the validity of my Darwinian theory. The souls that govern in our youth are so numerous and fractious that the records are confused. There are no permanent memories because they belong to the souls that perish.

I ARRIVED AT Princeton eager for my new life. I found that I made friends quickly with people on my hall, especially the girls. Every morning I would wake up filled with joy at the realization that I had been granted a reprieve from my years of painful growing and changing. Moreover, my professors were dazzled by my papers. No other freshman had read, for example, the entire corpus of Nietzsche's work. Or Augustine, Dante, Milton, Mann, Joyce—even most of *Finnegans Wake*.

Around me, the seasons seemed brand-new phenomena, so beautiful were they as they marched across the trees and gothic swards.

Lara, this was the directionless, intellectually hyperactive, socially ill-at-ease, emotionally inexperienced Andrew you discovered. Your face would break into a smile at something I said, and all that had occurred in my short, strange life seemed an episode in some novel dimly remembered from my youth. But now you're gone and I'm once again at the mercy of its tenebrous author. . . .

I RECENTLY READ that every action, every decision, splits the universe in two. In one resultant universe, choice A is made, in the other choice B. This is repeated ad nauseam for every decision ever made, including the "decisions" of apparently nonsentient particles governed by the dictates of quantum mechanics.

I have been dreaming lately of travel among these multiple universes. I've seen the vast panorama of universes that I inhabit. I've eavesdropped on versions of me in every possible permutation—movie star, famous composer, criminal mastermind, gas station attendant, Navy SEAL, pyromaniac, drug addict, masseur. I am the seer who sees into my infinite self.

I now understand that déjà vu is the awareness of the simultaneous occurrence of a nearly identical event in an alternative universe as perceived by another version of your self. That haunting sense of unreality and the flimsiness of time, of identity itself, is a window through which we glimpse another world.

I WAS WALKING across campus eating a turkey sandwich when I saw the person who would become the center and the end point of my life.

It was not, at first, her beauty that made me take notice. It was the certainty that I had seen her before.

I followed her with my eyes, trying to pin down where I knew her from. At the time I simply dismissed this as a bout of déjà vu. I did not ask the obvious question about the *meaning* of déjà vu. I now know it is a glimpse into the happenings of our alternative selves in alternative universes. Therefore she and I were together in other enactments of our lives. We were destined to meet and play out our version of the universal story.

I STOOD IN line at the Registrar's Office, waiting to sign up for spring semester classes. She joined the line about a dozen people behind me. I nonchalantly left the line and rejoined at the end, two people behind her. I watched the sheen of her blond hair, gorgeous and lush even under the fluorescent lights of the drab office. She reached the front of the line and for the first time I heard her say her name. I noted that she, Lara Anne Knowles, had registered for a psychology class, PSY 221.

I registered for the same class. We were orbiting the same sun, and the gravity was unstoppable.

Thinking that one day I would want to look back on the time she came into my life, I began to keep a diary.

Monday, February 3. First day of class. Saw Lara walk into lecture today, but she did not sit next to me. Professor Wernicke very tall.

Wednesday, February 5. Lara sat across lecture hall again. Wernicke announced that the ultimate goal of neurobiology was to determine the chemical basis of consciousness. What he is describing would be the greatest tragedy in human history. Drew a picture of Lara's profile. Stapled it to wall in room.

Monday, February 10. Found Lara's lab section on the listing outside the classroom and switched into her group. Wernicke took out a Tupperware container in mid-lecture and said it contained a piece of brain tissue. He took out the tissue and ate it. Only cantaloupe. Just a joke. Lara smiled but did not laugh.

Tuesday, February 11. First day of lab!

THERE WAS SOMETHING different in Lara's face. When you looked at her, there was no veil. No illusion or deception, only innocence and warmth. Her soul was mere millimeters beneath her skin. It would flare up and show itself in its eagerness to burst from this shallow confinement and commingle with the rest of us. Her soul had less restraint than bodies usually impose. She seemed to have been transplanted from another world, where love is made in public.

In Plato's *Symposium*, Aristophanes claims that each of us was originally joined to another person. For our time on earth we have been severed from our other half. We spend our lives searching for our counterparts. When we finally meet that other person, it is impossible to convey in words our happiness, our joy. We can think of nothing besides spending the rest of our lives with our match. "Love" is a name for a condition that re-creates our original wholeness.

—I'M NOT ACTUALLY supposed to be here, she said. There was a mix-up with the registrar. I can't be in this lab because of the animal experiments.

—Why did you sign up for the class?

—The professor said I could write a paper instead of being in the lab.

I looked at my notebook to collect my thoughts, to salvage my plan.

—You don't believe in using animals for medical research?

—In some cases it's necessary. Only if you can really learn something. Whatever I could hope to learn from fooling around with rats' brains is already known. I don't see any point in my butchering them.

She smiled at me, I suppose for no other reason than that I looked so perplexed. I needed to justify my presence in the class. How could I tell her my real purpose for being there had nothing to do with rats or psychology? It had to do with exactly what I was doing at that instant, holding the attention of Lara Knowles. Yet she was expecting some answer, some justification for the ease with which I could butcher rats. —I want to do research. Maybe someday I'll find a cure for a terrible disease.

By now the rest of the class was dribbling in. Lara approached the lab instructor and explained her situation. She waved at me as she left. Someone handed me a squealing white rat, held by the tail and somersaulting in fright.

THE BEST-LAID PLANS of rats and Andrew! How was I supposed to become closer to my darling without the pretext of lab work? It would have been so easy. Hi, Lara, it's Andy from psych lab. I was wondering if you knew whether the dopamine lab is due this week or next week? This week? Thanks. By the way, how are you doing?

I was left to more conventional methods. At least the rats had given me a way to introduce myself: Andrew Wallace, future neuroscientist, slayer of vermin. All I had to do was approach her at the student center and say, Remember me? I couldn't. I couldn't. I followed her around campus and tried dozens of times to approach her, but her beauty and her personality were overwhelming. I feared to come near them, much as space travelers must shy away from the sun. My days were a constant ecstasy of anticipation and cowardice, followed closely by reproachment, resolution and further anticipation.

Finally, one day I sat next to her in the dining hall and stammered:

—Weren't you in my psychology lab for about five minutes?

She closed her book and looked at me.

—Sure. You're the future winner of the Nobel Prize for your cure of Alzheimer's disease.

She drank her coffee. I offered my name and she told me hers. As if I didn't by that time already know her name, her address, her phone number, her birthday, all better than my own!

—If you don't want to do research, what do you want to be? I asked.

—Nothing. Everything.

—Humor me.

—Maybe a lawyer.

—A lawyer? You seem too pleasant.

—That's a sexist thing to say. If I were a guy you would never have said that.

—That's not true. I think I'm too pleasant to be a lawyer.

—Then you're conceited.

—You know, I take it back. I think you *would* make a good lawyer.

All this passed rapidly. We were actors running through familiar lines. We leaned toward each other and the room seemed to go quiet around us. Everyone else had stopped their conversations to listen.

Oh, God, if You exist, maybe You will let me live in that instant forever and ever, all time reduced to the dangerous look in her eyes and the movement of her slender index finger absently caressing the handle of the coffee mug.

The book she had been reading was unfamiliar to me, although I had of course heard of the author, Horace Jacob Little. The title was *Strange Meeting.*

—I'm just reading for fun. I think Horace Jacob Little is amazing. Have you ever read anything of his?

—He's an "idea" writer, right? Very postmodern? I prefer emotional involvement in the characters.

—Like a Victorian novel. Orphans, governesses, urban squalor, unlikely coincidences, marriages at the end?

She was playing with me. I couldn't believe how well the conversation was going. I wanted to avoid saying the wrong thing, negating all I had accomplished.

—I'd like to read more Horace Jacob Little, I said.

To my eternal delight, she answered:

—I'll lend you the book.

She got up to leave with the grace she imparted to every movement, sliding sideways out of her chair rather than simply standing.

—Call me when you want to return it.

I WAS WRONG to have dismissed Horace Jacob Little. The book was brilliant. It seemed to speak directly to me. Reading the stories in *Strange Meeting* was like looking into mirrors placed so as to create an infinite regression of images. I read it over and over, the words and ideas exploding in my mind. I could soon quote passages by heart. Embedded in that text was the secret to Lara's soul, and her scattered annotations and underlinings were directions on a treasure map of maddening obscurity. If Lara admired this writer as much as I did— well, so much more evidence that we were meant for each other.

chapter four

Not wanting to appear unenthusiastic to Fogerty, I called my old roommate George to ask for more detailed suggestions about how to find Horace Jacob Little. He said he couldn't talk because he was preparing his new place for a housewarming party.

"In fact, it's a good thing you called. You should come over tonight. It'll be some scene."

I admit to having felt slightly superior to George during college, when he epitomized the computer geek. I expected his party to take place in a small, unfurnished room, and the guests to consist mostly of fellow gaming or programming fanatics. I had not been in touch with him since graduation, so I was unaware of how things had changed.

George was raking in enormous sums of money working for a Wall Street company I had never heard of. His apartment turned out to be a cavernous and trendy loft in TriBeCa, filled with leather furniture and oversized abstract paintings, and this night packed with people to the point of oppression.

George met me at the door. "Hey, Jake!" he said, shaking my hand enthusiastically. I gave him the six-pack I had brought along.

George broke into a mock Gregorian chant, in honor of our old dorm, the Monastery. He shook my hand again, throwing his other arm around my shoulder. He had been made giddy by the number of people who had shown up at his party. He had also, it seemed, had a few drinks.

I examined a small framed drawing near the door, a woman's head exploded into different parts and angles. It had Picasso's signature on the bottom.

"That's not really a . . ." I said.

George nodded and looked at the picture intently, as if noticing it in his apartment for the first time.

"My company just transferred me here from the San Francisco office. I only moved in a few days ago. They gave this place to me, decorated and everything. A step up from the Monastery, right?"

"What exactly do you do?" I asked. "I know it's a computer thing, but what?"

He hesitated, apparently unsure whether I would understand anything technical. "I'm writing programs to help people know what trades to make."

A new group of guests arrived, and George excused himself to greet them. I scanned the room. I knew that in Manhattan, money found expression in the form of raw, unadulterated space. The empty air above buildings was worth sums beyond understanding. George's apartment was reminiscent of an airport hangar and therefore, even if a bit shabby, was a demonstration of great wealth. I couldn't help thinking, with a desire that was new to me, that I wanted that success, that money, that apartment.

I had looked around Manhattan for a place I could afford on my salary from the *Ledger*, which was less a realistic sum than a polite gesture toward remuneration. Through friends of my parents I found an old couple in Queens, Vinnie and Bea Cafarella, who had a second home in Fort Lauderdale. They were looking for someone to watch their apartment and baby-sit their cat, Jimmy. Once the Cafarellas determined that I was unlikely to set the place ablaze or let Jimmy starve to death, they rented the place to me for a song. As I marveled at George's loft, I was embarrassed by my own modest situation. What was I doing bumming around at a down-and-out newspaper?

I opened a beer and took a few sips. I noted the people I knew around the room, some of whom I had not spoken to since Princeton. They were arrayed in semi-darkness, lit by candles scattered around the apartment, and it seemed a convention of ghosts conjured by my memory in the freedom of sleep. People with whom I had done chemistry homework, old lab partners, fellow reporters from the *Daily Princetonian*—people I dreamed about and forgot, and who appeared to exist only because I once dreamed them.

Across the room, I saw Lara, my chief ghost, my memory's masterwork. And she saw me.

"Jake!" she said, leaping up from the couch. She had been sitting next to a guy in a tie and shirtsleeves who regarded me with suspicion. He was leaning back with his chin raised slightly, an aloof posture announcing to the rest of the room that she was already his.

"I want you to meet Glen Thaler," Lara said. "Glen, this is Jake Burnett, an old friend of mine."

Glen stood, raised his arm and shook my hand with a firm grip, a clasp that offered challenge rather than greeting. I knew the name from laying out the sports pages of the *Princetonian*, which often went on at great length about him and his fellow lacrosse players. They won a national championship during my last year at the paper.

"You were at Princeton?" Glen asked.

"Lara lived in my dorm freshman year."

"The Monastery?" he said, and looked to Lara for confirmation. She smiled in reply.

"What have you been up to?" I asked her.

"Law school," she said. "Like I always told you. I'm at NYU. I suppose you're the latest hotshot correspondent for *The Economist*. Or no, even better, you're writing an epic poem."

I smiled. "You got me. I figured, if Milton could do it . . ."

Glen was following this like a spectator at a tennis match, and it must have been dawning on him that Lara and I had once been more than dormmates or casual acquaintances.

"Milton!" Lara squealed. "Remember Professor Roberts? I haven't thought about him in forever. I got more sleep in his class than I did in my bed that semester."

"Which class was that?" Glen asked.

"Jake and I took a course on *Paradise Lost* sophomore year. We always joked that one of us would revive the genre of the epic poem."

"Not that it deserves reviving," Glen said.

"Would you get me a gin and tonic, hon?" Lara asked Glen. He nodded and departed. She turned her attention back to me. "Seriously, what have you been doing since graduation? Tell me absolutely everything."

"I went to Europe and traveled around. I was a paralegal at home for a while and I moved here a few weeks ago. I'm working at *The Manhattan Ledger*."

"My favorite newspaper. I consider it the paper of record."

I realized how glad I was to see her. She could have said, "The Manhattan what?" or simply ignored the matter. Instead she let fly a flattering absurdity. It captured what I used to love most about her— the way her generosity and wit skimmed over the world like dragon-flies above a lake, looking for a place to settle.

"You look fantastic," I said, and this was not a flattering absurdity. Lara seemed to have made her selection of evening wear directly from the pages of *Vogue*. No more jeans and sweats and hair scrunchies, which she had nevertheless managed to invest with a careless grace. At George's party she wore a black silk blouse, which fit like her own skin, and a memorably short skirt. Her straw-colored hair was pulled back into a tight bun, which gave her a sleek, cool bearing. Her beauty was an aggressive force, exercising a claim over my thoughts, demanding access to my most secret fantasies. I had never seen her wear an outfit so revelatory, or in a pose so sexual and commanding.

Glen returned, bearing a gin and tonic in a small plastic cup.

"Listen, I just ran into Joel Miller from Ivy over there," he said. "You'll excuse me for a minute."

He gave me a look that contained a hint of warning. I watched his broad back move through the room, as if toward a net through a crowd of defenders, and I remembered why his name was familiar. He had been caught by the town police smoking pot on the street. The university's regulations required a disciplinary hearing, but this was delayed until after lacrosse season so that Glen could continue to play. We ran a scathing editorial in the *Prince* about both the stupidity of doing drugs in public and the favoritism accorded to star athletes by the university. Our voice-mailbox was filled with violent and obscene messages from athletes for weeks after the editorial ran. Glen even came by the office in person to call us a bunch of fucking faggots.

"What does Glen do?" I asked.

"He's an I-banker."

"I was sorry to hear about you and Andrew Wallace."

She nodded and her gaze lost its sharpness. Her attention had turned inward. She nodded again, as though unaware she had already done so. I was sorry I had brought it up. All I could do was wait for her to recover, to make a little self-deprecating jibe and laugh it off. Instead she looked around the room anxiously.

"Let's sit down," she said, setting off for the nearby couch. I sat next to her.

"Is everything all right?"

"I had one of those moments when all of a sudden nothing seems real. Seeing you, thinking of Andy. All these memories . . ."

"Tell me more about law school."

"I just finished my first year. It's stupefyingly boring."

"But you always wanted to be a prosecutor. What about putting rapists in jail?"

"What about it? They get out on parole in six months. I'm probably going to do corporate law."

"Really." I didn't hide my astonishment. I had never seen Lara so bitter.

She gave me a wan smile. "I don't know what's gotten into me. It's been kind of tough getting back on track after Andy. I thought he and I were in it for the long haul, but you know—he got sick, and then he was gone."

"What do you mean?" I asked.

"He began having problems."

I had no idea what this meant. Problems with school? With drugs? With the law? I understood she wished to leave it indefinite.

"I didn't know," I said.

"How could you have? You hardly spoke to me after Andy and I started going out."

"That's not true. Or maybe it is, but it's certainly not my fault."

"Oh, it's mine?"

Glen appeared and said, "Hey, Jane Crocker is over here. Come say hi."

Lara rolled her eyes and sighed. She took Glen's outstretched hands and allowed herself to be lifted off the couch.

"Excuse me," she said, still sounding annoyed. "I have to go say hi to an old ego."

I watched her cross the room with Glen in the lead. They reached a group of five standing by the wall. A tall girl with black hair screeched and pressed her cheek to Lara's. She whispered in Lara's ear, and Lara laughed gamely. There was something horribly false about it all. Other partygoers blocked my view, and Lara's voice faded into the greater noise.

I drank my beer. I was in no mood to enjoy the rest of the party. I overheard someone near me talking about George's job, which, it turned out, involved creating computer models to predict the future of the stock market. It struck me as ironic that George—George Faber, who used to program his computer to troll the Internet for the first porn sites and who started an official campus organization concerned with all aspects of Martian Slaughter—was telling corporate titans where to put their money.

I found him and pulled him away from a cluster of people. He put his arm around my shoulder and said, "My long-lost roommate." He was very drunk.

"I need to ask you something," I said. "Maybe this isn't the best time."

"Isn't the best time?" He was incredulous. "What better time could there be?"

"I need you to help me find Horace Jacob Little."

He furrowed his brow and thought for a moment. His face brightened. "The author!" he said. "Sure, I remember. We'll hunt him down like a dog in the street."

"I don't think—"

"Nonsense," he said, and repeated the dog-in-the-street business, obviously pleased with himself. I sat him down and said, "Good night. I hope no one steals your Picasso. Are you okay?"

"I'm okay. I'm great."

As I reached the door, someone touched my arm.

"A bunch of us are going to a club in a while," Lara said, slipping her body around mine and blocking my exit. "Why don't you come with us?"

"I'm not really in the mood."

"Come on. It'll be fun. They'll be playing Strauss's latest waltz."

I laughed. She seemed to have recovered from her somber mood, but there remained a wary look in her eyes, an edge in her voice.

"It was great to see you," I said, and headed for the street.

I was still new to New York, and I didn't yet trust the subway late at night, so I grabbed a taxi. In the cab, I thought about the day I first met Lara. She was moving her belongings from her family's Mercedes station wagon into her room at the beginning of the year, and every male in the Monastery ran downstairs to help. We argued among ourselves about who would get to carry the heaviest stuff. She was so beautiful, and young and naive. I would never have foreseen that five years later she would be dating one of the more contemptible members of our class and on the road to a lifetime of corporate law. It was such a waste. As the cab crossed the Fifty-ninth Street Bridge, I watched the city bristling luminously behind me. I wished that I hadn't seen her, that she could have endured in my memory as an unfulfilled promise from the time when anything was possible for the monks and the nuns.

CHAPTER FIVE

After George's party I was drawn to thoughts of my past with Lara. In the intervening years I had purposefully blotted out her influence, but seeing her again uncovered a cache of indelible memories. The meeting made me realize that I had let something wonderful slip away, and that I had spent years waiting in vain for its replacement.

On a chilly November evening, during our first year at Princeton, Lara and I were walking back from the dining hall in the dark. The sky was a deep blue band, limited by the poles of Witherspoon and Joline.

"You mean you're not going home for Thanksgiving?" Lara said, shocked.

"It's a long way to go for a couple of days."

"Is everything okay at the Burnett homestead?"

"Sure."

"You're just going to hang around here?"

"Work on some papers. Maybe I'll go see a few museums in New York."

"That sounds miserable. Why don't you come home with me to Connecticut?"

"I don't want to barge in on your family's Thanksgiving."

"No, I mean it. It'll be fun."

I was an ordinary kid from Minneapolis, on heavy financial aid, and she was old Protestant stock from New England. Her family's men had gone to Harvard for generations, stretching back to the early nineteenth century. It had been a big deal in her house when she decided to defect to Princeton. Lara never made an issue of money, but I still felt ambivalent about going to Greenwich for Thanksgiving. The last thing I wanted was for her to see me as a charity case. Still, she invited me with such enthusiasm that I couldn't have said no, even if I had wanted to.

Her parents had left a car with her at school, a hunter-green BMW with tan leather upholstery.

"Welcome to the Waspmobile," Lara said after we hiked down to the lot at the foot of campus.

"Nice car," I said.

"I think it's embarrassing. I wanted to buy a used Toyota or something."

It was dusk as we drove up Route 1 toward the New Jersey Turnpike. I searched for an acceptable radio station as she drove. She would park herself in the slow lane for five minutes until she became frustrated with the pace, and then she would gun the engine, swing into the fast lane and do ninety for several minutes before returning to the slow lane to begin the cycle again.

"I want to warn you," she said. "My parents recently separated. They insisted we spend Thanksgiving all together, though."

"Are you worried?"

"I don't want you to be uncomfortable."

"We're close enough to Princeton to turn around."

"No, I really want you to meet them. It'll be fun to spend time with you without having to worry about school."

I tuned past country, talk, pop, oldies, R&B, adult contemporary.

"All this music sucks," she said. "I think there are tapes in the glove compartment."

I located a battered tape labeled "Wagner" and put it in the player.

"Now, *this* is good." She turned the volume up until the superiority of the stereo system became apparent. We were hurtling down the fast lane, passing the more timid cars every few seconds. The sun disappeared behind the weathered mountains of the Eastern Seaboard. The Wagner was so loud we could not have heard each other without shouting. I thought, *She is like no one I have ever met.*

Lara's house, in a neighborhood of palatial homes, was huge and beautiful, a white colonial with green shutters. There was already a thin dusting of snow on the lawn, which rolled down to the street, ending at a tall hedge in the distance. Lara's father had moved out, leaving only Mrs. Knowles to live in the house. It would have been too large even for the three of them. To live alone in such a mansion seemed to me ridiculous.

Mrs. Knowles met us in the kitchen and fixed us tea. The room was lined with metal appliances and professional-looking cabinets. A serious chef would have been happy to work there. Mrs. Knowles was not a serious chef, but a serious lawyer for a corporation in Stamford. From her Lara had inherited her looks, and possibly her intelligence.

"It's wonderful to have you here, Jake. In this family we get bored of each other rather easily."

"Thanks, Mom," Lara said. "Great to be home."

"You look tired, sweetie," Mrs. Knowles said. She reminded me of the women who model for fashion magazines—beautiful and haughty, yet vaguely solicitous.

"It was a long drive," Lara said, pulling the sleeves of her sweater over her hands. Mrs. Knowles stroked her daughter's long blond hair.

"You're in the Monastery, too?" she asked me.

"It's a great dorm."

"My daughter the monk." She turned to Lara. "How's your roommate?"

"Fine," Lara said. "We had a disagreement about closet space last week, but everything's okay."

"I understand she's something of a party girl," Mrs. Knowles said to me. "I think Lara should take advantage of this. Go out drinking with Karen. Dance until dawn."

"Do you believe this?" Lara said. "I have the worst parents in the world. God knows how I turned out normal."

Mrs. Knowles planted a kiss on her daughter's forehead. I excused myself to go unpack, thinking they had a lot to talk about.

MR. KNOWLES HAD moved into an apartment close to the courthouse where he worked as a judge. When he arrived for dinner Lara gave him a hug, I shook his hand, and Mrs. Knowles stood across the room.

"Hello, Henry," she said, at which he nodded.

Lara's father was from an old, grand family and had a patrician ease about him. It appeared nothing could worry him. He had a way of dropping his voice that made it seem he was telling you great secrets. Acting like we were old friends, he joined me as I watched a football game on television. He commented on it dispassionately, as one might discuss an opera seen a few weeks previously.

"Wonderful block there . . . Beautiful pass."

Thanksgiving dinner took place in a large dining room with a window facing the backyard pool, which was jacketed for the season. The pool was the last thing visible as night fell. The table, under an immense chandelier, was set with gorgeous china and an explosion of dried flowers as a centerpiece. I half expected domestics to emerge from the kitchen bearing wine and food, but Mrs. Knowles brought in the turkey, and Mr. Knowles carved it. A fire crackled in a fireplace in the corner of the room.

"To health, life and peace," Mr. Knowles said as a toast. "We are thankful for what we have."

Mrs. Knowles gave her husband a sarcastic look. Lara had told me that her father was the one who thought the marriage wasn't working. He was seeing a paralegal from the Prosecutor's Office.

"And to family," Mrs. Knowles said, her voice as hard as the glass she held. I wondered whether my presence at the table was the only thing keeping everyone civil, and whether Lara had invited me specifically for that purpose.

"Your mother tells me you're not getting along with your roommate," Mr. Knowles said to Lara, apparently glad to be done with the awkward toasting.

"Everything's okay," Lara replied. "We're not best friends, that's all."

"You live in that dorm, right?" he asked me. "Do you know Karen?"

"Sure. She's a little crazy. Did you tell your parents about—"

Lara kicked me under the table.

"About what?" Mr. Knowles sounded like the judge he was.

"Last week Karen hung a sweater too close to the halogen lamp," Lara said. "It caught on fire and I had to put it out."

Her parents put down their silverware and leaned forward. The reaction was immediate, instinctual. They had forgotten the circumstances of the family reunion.

"My God," Mr. Knowles said.

"Oh, honey," Mrs. Knowles said. "Are you okay? You didn't get hurt, did you?"

"It was no big deal. I stomped it out. The sweater was acrylic, though. It kind of melted and released horrible fumes. I had to spend two nights in my friend Lisa's room."

In truth, she had stayed on the futon in my common room, a fact I was glad she didn't bring up in front of her parents. Her proximity that night had been torture to me.

"I'm not happy with this," Mr. Knowles said. "It's one thing to have arguments. It's quite another to set the room on fire."

"Why didn't you tell me?" her mother said. "When we were talking about Karen yesterday."

Lara looked at me, reproachfully. I asked her to pass the turkey.

Lara's parents inquired about my family, about Minneapolis, about what I was studying at Princeton. I was eager to please them.

"Okay, enough of the third degree, guys," Lara said. "I want to hear more about this case Dad's hearing."

"It's a barroom fight that ended with someone killed by a blow to the head with a chair. The grand jury indicted on murder two, but—"

"I don't think this is the place to talk about murder and mayhem," Mrs. Knowles said.

"Come on, Mom. You want me to be a lawyer, don't you?"

"Not at the Thanksgiving table, I don't."

Conversation came to a halt. In a normal family Mrs. Knowles's words would have been forgotten or smoothed over, but at that table the silence lingered and lengthened. What was uncomfortable for me must have been excruciating for Lara, who sat across from me pouring gravy, stoic and beautiful.

"CHECK IT OUT," Lara said, coming into the cozy guest room where I was staying. She carried a small stuffed tiger with an orange "P" on its chest. "My mom left this in my room."

She sat next to me on the bed. "My dad was pretty upset that I decided not to go to Harvard, but my mom told me I should go wherever I thought I'd be happy. She left me a little tiger to show me she's proud of me."

Even her choice of college had become a point of contention between her parents, a competition for influence and love. I had a feeling such skirmishes were just beginning.

"What's the difference?" I said. "Harvard, Princeton."

"That's a great attitude. I'm sure Dean FitzRandolph would be thrilled. Harvard is a family tradition. My dad was disappointed for about a week, then he got over it. I guess they have bigger problems now. What are you reading?"

"A Horace Jacob Little book. *Strange Meeting.*"

"I've never read anything by him."

"He's my favorite author."

I gave her the book and she paged through it.

"Why is the cover blank? Where are all the blurbs and stuff?"

"He doesn't allow them. He's a total recluse. No one even knows what he looks like."

She wrinkled her brow. "Sounds like a publicity stunt."

"It's been going on for twenty years. I'm giving you this book, okay? It's yours. I guarantee you'll love it."

She put the book next to the tiger.

"I'm glad you're here," she said. She looked at the tiger, which appeared to anger her. "It's final. My parents are getting divorced. My mom told me yesterday. You couldn't tell, could you? They're two great actors. I swear to God, they could do Shakespeare."

"I'm sorry," I said. To have put on such a show for Lara, and yet to know that she was well aware it was only a show—it required a degree of self-control I could hardly imagine. Parents of friends of mine had gotten divorced and ended up poisoning the kids against the enemy spouse. I thought of how Mr. Knowles, leaving after dinner, had stood for a full minute with his car door open, staring at the house. Everything in Lara's life that had been an advantage—her parents' money, their hopes for her, the perfection of the house—seemed poised to turn against her and become oppressive. I wanted to take her away from there.

"I'm glad you're here," she repeated, this time in a whisper, and moved toward me.

"What about your mom?" I said.

"She's in a different part of the house." She pushed the tiger and the book off the bed. I put my hand around her waist, under the edge of her shirt. A better person might have pulled away, realizing that she was upset and maybe looking for some sort of comfort. But someone who had dreamed of feeling the smooth skin of her back and the hard strap of her bra, who was overwhelmed simply by her scent as she entered a room, who was, in short, in love for the first time, would not have pulled away. The idea would not have occurred to him.

LARA SPENT THE next semester in Paris. She called me in late January from her hostel, just after arriving.

"I'm scared," she said. "I've never felt this way before. I barely speak the language. I miss Princeton. I miss you. Jesus, I even miss Karen."

"You'll do great," I said, miserably. "Within a week you'll be having full conversations with people."

"Impossible."

"Buying baguettes on the Champs-Élysées."

"I wish."

She e-mailed me two or three times a week, and I answered. We sent handwritten letters back and forth, believing that the old-fashioned way was a more meaningful method of communication. Soon she was writing about what a wonderful time she was having, about the great friends she had made at school. There was less and less about how much she missed me. Without her, Princeton was a joyless place.

When can I come visit you? I wrote.

Anytime, she replied.

I feel like you've taken to Paris everything good about this place. There's nothing left here worth anything.

I just got back from the Loire Valley. We rented bikes and rode twenty-three miles! You should have seen the fields of sunflowers and the old châteaux. It's a wonder I didn't kill myself, since I was never watching the road.

Karen's new roommate has moved out already. I don't know how you got along with her.

It seems that all that stuff with Karen happened years ago.

I'm getting tired of working at the *Prince*. All these stupid articles that no one really reads anyway. It isn't fun anymore.

I had the greatest day yesterday. I went down to the Seine to watch the sunset and met a friend for dinner at this tiny café near

Notre-Dame. I want to live here after graduation. Every little gesture, every detail of life that's a chore at home is transformed here
into something wonderful. I never want to leave! By the way, when
are you coming to visit?

Anytime.

I LOOKED LARA up as soon as I received the campus phone book at
the start of sophomore year. I went by Witherspoon, where she had a
single, and knocked on her door.

"Jake!" she shouted. "Oh my God."

We hugged.

"It's been a long time," I said. Her hair was short, a boyish cut.
She wore a long flowered skirt. She still looked beautiful, and now
more sophisticated. Paris had rubbed off on her.

"Were you going out?" I asked.

"Yes. I'm going with you to get some coffee."

We walked over to the old student center, where we took two
plush easy chairs on the second floor of the dark rotunda. Groups of
nervous freshmen surrounded us.

"Nothing's changed around here," she said.

"You've only been gone a semester."

"It seems like much longer. I have to tell you all about my trip
down through Italy over the summer."

"How are your parents?"

"The divorce is done. They're both seeing other people."

"That must be hard."

She drank her coffee, and left a rich maroon lipstick stain on the
white plastic cover of the cup.

"I understand why they wanted me to go abroad. If I had been
around here and going home every weekend I would have been a

mental wreck. Being away, I feel like I have a new perspective. I love them both and I want them to be happy."

"It's great to see you. I really missed you."

She pressed her lips together. "If things had worked out differently, I think we could have really had something together."

I swirled my coffee in its cup, hating the past tense. I had never fully understood our status with regard to each other. Were we best friends who happened to sleep together several times? Were we more than that? Less? We were getting together that night to compose a valediction for our indefinite relationship.

"I feel like I'm a different person," she said. "I always assumed I would go to Princeton, become a lawyer and live like my parents did. Now I have these wild fantasies of moving back to Paris to write, or becoming a social worker on an Indian reservation or something. I have a million new ideas. I don't think I'm ready for a big relationship."

I had nurtured fantasies that we would fall madly in love upon her return. I thought there must have been words I could say, actions I could perform that would make her change her mind. I had never felt as useless and unprepared for life as I did at that moment.

"It's still good to see you," I said.

"By the way, I'm now the world's biggest Horace Jacob Little fan. I found an English bookstore in Paris and kept buying his books. He's very popular over there. They love that he lives *sous l'anonymat*."

The next day, I saw Lara across McCosh Walk at dusk. I almost ran after her to say hello, but instead I set my pace to match and followed her. I did not wonder where she was going. I did not wish to check up on her. I only wanted to keep watching her for a few minutes.

LARA BEGAN HANGING out with a new crowd that was centered around 2D, the campus vegetarian co-op. If there was a bastion of radicalism at Princeton, 2D was it. Bearded guys in socks and sandals stalked around speaking of the military-industrial complex and the ideas of Noam Chomsky. Girls with bandannas around their hair wrote poetry about Mother Earth and Sister River.

Occasionally Lara and I would meet as we walked across campus. Our encounters were fraught with awkwardness, and they invariably ruined my day. We would mumble about classes, the weather. We would interrupt each other and wait in silence for the other to continue. Even if we had been fluent and thrilled to see one another, we no longer had much in common to talk about. She was in 2D and had her own group. I was practically living at the *Prince*.

I tried to keep track of Lara on the sly, through information gleaned from friends we had in common. I heard, from George, that Lara was going out with Andrew Wallace, a 2D member. He had lived in the building next to the Monastery during freshman year. His most memorable feature was the unruly brown hair that fell around his ears and in front of his forehead. He had a thin, handsome face, and wire-framed glasses rested on his aristocratic nose. I had passed him on campus paths dozens of times, but we had never been introduced. He dressed in vintage clothes, old bell bottoms, short-sleeved buttondown shirts. He always looked to me like a hipster intellectual, someone who would play bass in a rock band and go home to read the work of obscure German philosophers.

Toward the end of junior year, I wandered into a 2D party. Co-op members had made their own wine, flavored with tart raspberry, and they were in the process of consuming it. In the darkened living room of the house, the whole crew had gathered in a circle on the floor. Some people played bongos, drums and flutes, while others hummed and chanted. People took turns at vocal solos, improvisational exercises. The smell of pot and cigarettes and sweet wine hung thickly in the room. Lara was leaning on Andrew, who was banging a drum with intense concentration, his long hair covering his face. The time came for her to sing.

She stood, and sang beautifully.

CHAPTer SIX

FROM THE *CONFESSIONS* OF ANDREW WALLACE

Incompatible temperatures coated the coffee shop window with a layer of steam. From the outside I could see only the blurred shapes and colors of coats and tables. I opened the door to the overwhelming scent of roasting coffee beans and a humid heat that stung my cold skin. I was momentarily bewildered by the temperature, the smell, the noise, the emptiness below my heart, the excessive activity of that organ, the steam that was forming on my glasses and covering the world in a bleary whiteness. I was there for a date with Lara, really my first date ever, and my senses were dangerously overstimulated. I removed my glasses and wiped them on my shirtfront, calming, calming. I replaced them and found her sitting at a small table in a corner, her legs crossed, the dangling foot dancing. The way she was looking at me, I might have been the only person in the room, in the world, in the universe.

—Did you bring my book? she said.

—Of course.

—Which story was your favorite?

—"Strange Meeting." It reminded me so much of Borges.

—I lovvvve Borges. I may write my thesis on him.

This led to a romp through the infinite library and around the Aleph. There was a deep symmetry behind our conversation. The stories we discussed were surrogates for a subtext. There we were, two future comparative literature majors, talking excitedly of writers and words. But it was a code. We were really talking about ourselves.

Lara paged through the book. She said:

—All the stories in *Strange Meeting* involve insanity. Like in the title story. It's interesting. Before *Strange Meeting* came out, most of Horace Jacob Little's writing was relatively sedate and poetic. After this it takes a U-turn—it's all about ideas and riddles and madness.

—Nobody knows who he is, so we can't ask him about it.

I was afraid to pick up my coffee. I thought I might spill it on myself, or on her, or make a clatter as my trembling hand brought the mug back to the table.

—We don't want to talk just about Horace Jacob Little, do we? She leaned forward to continue the discussion on a higher plane of intimacy.

I didn't. I certainly didn't. A warm glow was arising from her and extending outward into space, encompassing us in an aura of peace and stillness that was already my new reason for living.

—I noticed the name on the inside cover. Jake Somebody.

—That's the guy who gave me the book. My old boyfriend, I guess you could call him.

—Were you together long?

I saw the indecision flash through her eyes. I had forced the issue. Would this end here, a nice discussion with a friendly classmate about a book? Or would she proceed, and lead me into the labyrinth of her past? I watched her decide the course of my future.

—This was back in freshman year, when my parents were getting divorced. . . .

And we stayed there until they closed the place on us.

I LOOK BACK on those days with envy for my past happiness. I was in love with Lara, and she with me. I had found 2D, the campus vegetarian co-op, which was a world apart from Princeton. Where Princeton was elitist, 2D was egalitarian. Where Princeton was conformist, 2D was eccentric. I loved that place, and every day I wish I could leave this Muse Asylum and return to it.

I discovered 2D almost by chance (as if there is such a thing as chance). Walking down University Place to the Wa-Wa market for some soda, I passed two guys on the porch of a house arguing about the existence of the external world.

—Why stop with the material world? I shouted from the sidewalk. What about time? If you can't prove the reality of that tree, on what basis can you prove the existence of time?

They invited me in for dinner. It was a vegetarian feast. Black-bean-and-rice casserole, tofu lasagna, bowls and bowls of pasta salads. The members of the co-op wore tie-dyed shirts and ripped pants, sandals and unmatched socks. These were people who were too odd and interesting to fit into the mainstream of life at Princeton, and they made me comfortable and happy. They would not look at me askance if I did not shave, if I walked around with my hair uncombed. It was like finding an instant family.

Lara also fit into the alternative 2D universe. Her parents had always wanted her to be a lawyer. She was realizing there was more to

life than a good job and a cushy home in the country. Need I add that
her parents disapproved of this interest in 2D, and moreover disapproved of me? That was fine, because I disapproved of them too.

She got into the spirit of the place at her first dinner there,
needling me about experiments I was doing for Professor Wernicke. I
had taken his psychology class only to get closer to Lara, but I came
to be intrigued by the subject. Professor Wernicke asked me to test a
new putative antidepressant for my final lab report. I jumped at the
chance. It involved injecting the chemical into rats' brains and
throwing the rats into a swimming pool with walls too slick to cling
to or climb. The longer the rats swam before giving up and sinking,
supposedly, the less depressed they were. This was the Forced Swim
Test.

Lara thought this was barbaric.

—You let them drown?

—No, of course not. As soon as they give up, we reach in and take
them out.

—Still, you bring them to the edge of death.

—I don't know if it's the edge of death.

Everyone at the dinner table agreed with her. I chewed my baked
ziti, glad to be the center of Lara's attention.

—This whole science is cruel, said Sarah Klein, another student
in Wernicke's class. Did you read the part in our textbook about sleep
deprivation? They put a cat on an island just big enough for him to
stand on. Whenever he fell asleep, he would lose his balance, fall in
the water and wake up. The cat never got any sleep, and he died.

—You don't think research into sleep is a good thing? I asked the
table at large. Why do we sleep? Why do we dream? These are things
I'd like to know.

I walked Lara back to her dorm room after dinner. She was vibrating with excitement.

—I love that place, she said. I can't believe I never went there before.

—We could sign up as members.

—Everyone living under the same roof, pitching in to make the food and get things done. I can hear my father now: You mean my daughter is living in a *commune?*

—Should we try to get in?

—Absolutely.

We won the lottery and moved to the house on University Place. Housing was not officially coed, but I had a room next door to Lara's. We made my room into a study and living area. Lara's was the bedroom for us both.

We became as one. We got up together, fixed each other toast and coffee in the co-op kitchen, thought about each other during the morning, reunited for lunch at the student center, visited each other at Firestone Library in the afternoon, helped cook dinner at 2D and stayed up late talking and studying, then listened to music as we drifted off to sleep. Sometimes Lara would not be able to sleep and she would wake me up. I would read to her from our favorite books, including *Strange Meeting.* She left notes in my bag, which I would discover in the middle of a boring class. "I love you," they said. Or simply, "You." A single word that meant everything to us. I would not have changed the smallest detail of my life, or moved a single molecule the length of an angstrom.

I WAS SURPRISED to answer my phone one day and find Professor Wernicke on the other end.

—I have bad news. Your rat is dead, probably from an infection that set in after the implant surgery. Your final data may be incomplete. That's okay with me. You've already done more than enough work in the course.

I was less concerned with the possibility of losing data than with the killing of an innocent animal. I could justify the death of a lab subject in the abstract with no trouble, but Harvey had endeared himself to me over the course of the semester. He was there when I first spoke to Lara. He had urinated on my sleeve after she walked out of the room. Whenever I picked him out of the cistern during the Forced Swim Test, I imagined that he clung gratefully to me, his rescuer. He was disarmingly cute when I placed him, soaking wet and shivering, in front of a space heater to dry and fluff his fur.

Did he guess in his final moments of agony that I was responsible for his death? In retrospect, his death marked the first gentle assertion by mortality that all good things must end. Soon enough, for all practical purposes, I too would be dead.

TIME CAME TO settle on a topic for my senior thesis.

What else would I write about? Horace Jacob Little had been my password to love and happiness. My relationship with Lara was tangled up in his fiction. We had read together all his books. I loved to close my eyes and listen to her voice as she read his words to me. Her voice became softer and slower, and I always had the sensation that she was communicating on a level above or below speech. We argued about which of his books was best. If something in the real world resembled a detail from his work, we would look at each other and wink. It was almost an obligation on my part to write a thesis about Horace Jacob Little, whose words had formed the basis of our love.

I undertook that research with innocent intent. I only wished to praise him, to explicate an aspect of his work and thereby bring it greater glory. I did not know what I would find.

I decided to write about the story "Strange Meeting," which begins thus:

> Evan rode his bike down Sycamore Road, through thickets of the namesake trees, and up Pumpkin Hill, which had produced no pumpkins in a hundred years, until he arrived at the house that had been in the Small family for two centuries, a colonial-era house, built of pink bricks that had lost small crumbles of their edges to the storms and suns of the intransigent years. If you asked Seamus Small about a certain photograph from an earlier era, he would have shown you, with the genuine pleasure of a history-buff whose own home happened to be an artifact, a daguerreotype of the house and its contemporaneous Smalls, dour and scowling on the lawn.

Evan is the confused protagonist of the story, a not-so-swift student at the local boarding school, Magdalen Academy. Small, the retired headmaster, wants to interest Evan in the classics. He assigns great books for the boy to read and discuss with him. Evan would rather hang out with his friends, drinking and smoking.

On the day in question, Small wants to discuss Dante's *Inferno* with Evan. It is worth mentioning that "Strange Meeting" is divided into short sections, each of which is headed by a quotation, in Italian, from Dante. The discussion of the *Inferno* goes nowhere fast. In a section entitled "Come 'l mio corpo stea nel mondo su, nulla scïenza porto," Small asks Evan to bring him some fruit:

Evan stood and walked into the kitchen, which was notice-
ably colder than the fire-heated parlor. When he found no
fruit in the refrigerator, he checked the pantry, letting the
knotted wooden door swing shut slowly behind him with a
whining creak. The pantry was as cool as the night outside,
and Evan was in no hurry to return. He knew Small was
preparing another harangue.

Just as Evan found some soft pears the doorbell sounded.
Through the crack of the open pantry door, he could see
Small check his watch before removing the blanket from his
legs and rising to go to the front door. The hour was late, and
nobody ever interrupted their meetings. Evan was curious
about the unknown visitor.

The pantry door muffled the actual words, but Evan was
surprised to hear that the new voice sounded just like Small's.
The man walked into Evan's line of sight, and Evan began his
descent into a new world of confusion and strange visitations.

For he saw, with astonishment, that the visitor was an
identical twin to Small. They shared every detail of anatomy
and attire, from their faces to their height to the fuzzy red
slippers they were wearing.

The real Small sat in his recliner and said, "Do what you
must."

At that, the twin grasped Small's throat, as gently as a
mother touching a baby, and began strangling him. He lifted
Small out of the chair and held him so that his feet dangled
inches above the floor. Small emitted a final, low-pitched
groan. The twin let the body fall hard to the floor.

He dragged the body out the front door, holding it by the
hair. Evan heard a car engine start with a chortle. Headlights

swept around the parlor and the car drove down the pebbled driveway. The twin reentered the house, closed the door and sat down in Small's easy chair, wrapping himself in the blanket exactly as Small had swaddled himself only minutes before.

After an hour of reading the volume of Dante that had been left on the arm of the chair, the twin yawned and stretched. He went upstairs to bed with a ponderous stride that matched Small's. The house was quiet. Evan crept to the pantry window, climbed outside and ran for home, forgetting his bicycle against an ancient maple near the porch.

Evan begins to go mad, not sleeping, constantly thinking about this hallucination. Meanwhile, Small is seen around town acting strangely.

Finally, going through his copy of Dante, Evan opens to the thirty-third canto. He reads the words of Frate Alberigo, who claims that a soul may be sent to hell even in advance of death. In such a case, a devil ascends to earth and takes the place of the sinner.

Evan can't imagine what Small could have done to deserve this punishment. He is horrified by the unforgiving brand of justice. It occurs to him that the same fate may have befallen any number of people in town without anyone else's knowing it. He decides to avenge the death of his mentor by eliminating the twin. He shows up at the Small house. The twin says doctors have told him he is developing Alzheimer's disease. Evan understands that this is a clever way of disguising the twin's unfamiliarity with the real Small's habits and acquaintances. Evan stands behind the twin, who suspects nothing, and slits his throat with a kitchen knife.

The story ends with a section entitled "Per me si va nella città dolente":

Evan wandered into the post office to buy some stamps. He went to the drugstore to pick up a copy of the paper. He bought a cup of coffee and drank it as he walked down Main Street. Mrs. Logan smiled at him and waved hello. Across the street the Morehouses were getting out of their car. And Evan saw, with the slow-motion clarity usually reserved for dreams, someone with his own face turn the corner and catch sight of him.

At first I thought I would write about the connection between Dante and "Strange Meeting." My thesis advisor, Professor Linus Mullin, told me:

—"Strange Meeting" is Horace Jacob Little's attempt to reimagine Dante's *Inferno* as a contemporary American landscape. Why don't you see what you can come up with along those lines?

I labored diligently under this rubric, reading the Dante criticism, researching the story of Frate Alberigo, tracking down and translating the lines from the *Inferno* that Horace Jacob Little had lifted for section titles.

My breakthrough came from a different source, a book called *Names for Baby* that I found while browsing in the U-Store. It listed thousands of names and gave their derivations and meanings. Just for fun I looked up my name, which meant "manly." "Lara" was depicted by Ovid as a nymph whose tongue was cut out by Jupiter on account of her talkativeness. I couldn't wait to tease Lara about this.

I wondered if Horace Jacob Little, who had made "Strange Meeting" a giant puzzle of references, might have picked the names Evan Doherty and Seamus Small because of their etymologies.

"Evan" was derived from "John," and I couldn't think of any further significance. "Seamus" was related to "James," which was related to "Jacob."

As soon as I read that, I realized that "Small" was a synonym for "Little."

—TO MY KNOWLEDGE, no one has noticed this before, said Professor Mullin. It's interesting, but have you given any thought to what it means?

—I think it's obvious. "Strange Meeting" represents a drastic change in subject and style for Horace Jacob Little. No more mushy humanistic stories like in *The Length of New Jersey.* Suddenly he's a metaphysicist. It's as if he had been replaced by another writer. "Strange Meeting" is a story he wrote about *himself,* so he named the character after himself. It's his statement about the process of finding a new aesthetic.

Mullin was as excited as I was.

—I think it's fabulous, he said. I can't wait to see what else you come up with.

chapter seven

After George's party, Lara called me and invited me out for a drink. Actually, she didn't simply invite me—she said she *really* wanted to talk to me. I was curious about her urgency. After a frustrating day of playing phone tag with preoccupied city officials and assaulting the bulwark of silence that was the mayor's press office, I left the rundown offices of the *Ledger* and walked through crowded streets. It was not yet dark, and I could see low inflamed clouds over New Jersey, beyond the canyons between buildings. I was still unused to the city, to the rapid dance people performed to avoid one another on impassable midtown streets, to the wailing of sirens and horns, to the screeches of brakes from aggressive taxis. I wanted to love New York, but it grated on me.

Lara was at a table at the end of the room—a trendy place, Dive, whose name was apparently a play on its sophisticated decor. The bar looked like it was from the future, all metal and sheen, and the couches in the dim room would have been at home in a damp château. An upscale after-work crowd milled around the bar.

"Thanks for coming," Lara said.

She had been supremely confident at George's party, flush with the knowledge that her beauty and clothes and promising career were impressing me and everyone else. Now that aura of perfection had disappeared. She wore a baggy "Big P" Princeton sweatshirt and her hair needed attention. Her eyes were bloodshot. Despite all this, she was the most beautiful person in the place. I was proud to take a seat across from her.

She had ensconced herself in the darkest corner of the room. People at the bar were singing along to the pop song of the moment. "Wanna show ya the way to paradise, Wanna give ya a brand-new time and space, uh-huh . . ."

"Is everything all right?" I said.

"Do you remember the snowball fight?" There was concern across her face, as though much was riding on my answer.

"What snowball fight?"

"We were all walking back toward Blair East, and the quad in front of Witherspoon was this expanse of whiteness," she said, staring behind me. "All the tree branches were covered with ice and there was like two feet of snow. John Flood, out of nowhere, nailed George Faber with a snowball. That did it. Everyone started running around and pelting each other. Do you remember?"

"I remember. We all had hot chocolate afterward in the laundry room and waited for our clothes to dry, right?"

It was not a scene at the forefront of my memory, but at her mention the delicious experience came back to me: The feeling of unreality as the snow converted the world into a pristine version of itself.

Lara falling on top of me and into the new snow, laughing hysterically, as someone threw snowballs at her. The warmth of the laundry
room and the sweet smell of detergent as we talked about silly things
and the dryers hummed earnestly.

"I started thinking about the snowball fight after I saw you the
other night," she said. "It seems so long ago. Here's my question for
you. Will we ever have fun like that again? I mean running around
and laughing like a bunch of children?"

"Why not?"

This was clearly not about catching up with an old friend over
drinks. I couldn't then understand what she was trying to say: that
there had arisen a vast distance between the carefree games of freshman year, which included our brief relationship, and the adult problems she had been saddled with in the present.

"Hey, are you sure you're okay?" I asked again.

"I wanted you to meet me because I need advice. You and I
always seemed on the same wavelength. What I'm trying to say is,
I know we lost touch, but I trust your judgment."

She spoke quickly, each sentence necessary to qualify the previous, to make herself more clear. My curiosity and unease were growing. She had always existed in my mind as I had first known her in
the Monastery—vivid, untroubled, happy. I wanted her world to
remain perfect and uncorrupted. But at George's party she had been
miserable and annoyed. Now I found her so unsettled about something that she was willing to appeal for advice to me, someone she
had hardly seen in years. I wanted to help her, because I was still
capable of falling in love with her at any time.

"You know I went out with Andy Wallace a year and a half at
Princeton. Did you know him?"

"I knew who he was. We never really met."

"How can I describe Andy?" she asked the ceiling. "He was flat-out the most amazing person I have ever known. We met in a psych class, and the professor submitted Andy's final lab report to the journal *Brain*, which published it. That's Andy in a nutshell, incredibly brilliant. He wrote stories and plays as gifts for me on my birthday, on Valentine's Day. We were inseparable. We were going to travel around the world after graduation and get married a few years down the road."

I fought an impulse to change the subject. I was annoyed that she felt it important to praise the person she dated after deciding I wasn't good enough for her.

"Why are you telling me this?" I said.

"It started very slowly. His eccentricities became more pronounced at first. Here was someone who could pick up a pine cone and tell you about its natural history. He was different from everyone else. That's why I loved him. But slowly, he started being a little more different. People at 2D had all sorts of crazy theories about the government and the media. He began to take these things seriously."

"I always thought you went out with Andrew because he was so different from you. Same with you and the whole 2D crowd."

"What do you mean?"

I was sorry I had said anything, since Lara obviously was not interested in deconstructing her past behavior. Could I tell her that I resented the way she changed after she got back from France, and that I blamed 2D for her transformation? She became a budding amateur radical, dressing in long skirts and concealing her beautiful hair in tight braids. She expressed contempt, even hatred, for her parents. She was dating this Andrew person, who may have been brilliant but was also undeniably strange. At the time I couldn't even talk to her anymore. She wouldn't have understood anything I had to say.

"You wanted to do things your parents wouldn't approve of," I said. "So you lived with a houseful of eccentric people and dated a mysterious artist type."

She glared at me. "Maybe calling you was a bad idea."

"What—I'm wrong?"

"Yes, you're wrong. This has nothing to do with my parents. I loved Andy, period. I don't see why you need to sit here and come up with absurd theories."

She took a long drink from her bottle of beer, looking at me. Our unresolved emotions and resentments were presenting themselves, unbidden. I considered leaving, but I couldn't do it. I used to care for her so much that I couldn't pretend I no longer cared at all.

"What happened with Andrew?" I asked.

"One day he told me Professor Wernicke—our psych professor—was poisoning his lab rats. He would say people were following us when we walked around campus. He stopped going to classes. He stopped combing his hair and taking care of himself. He told me Horace Jacob Little was out to get him."

"Horace Jacob Little?"

There was that name again. It took me a second to realize that Lara didn't know of the article I was attempting to write about him, that my hope of finding him was still a secret desire.

"If you hadn't introduced me to Horace Jacob Little," she said, "I wouldn't have introduced Andy to him. Andy began his thesis on Horace Jacob Little, and it was like he couldn't get him out of his brain once he started it."

She took another sip of beer and went on. I wasn't listening. I was remembering her introduction to Horace Jacob Little—a stuffed tiger and *Strange Meeting* falling to her bedroom floor, forgotten. Lara was sliding toward me, running her hand up the side of my chest. I was finding the zipper of her pants and trying to contain myself enough to open its immobile mechanism.

"I don't know," Lara continued, unaware of my lapse of attention. "He would look at me like I was crazy for suggesting that something was wrong. Do you remember Dennis Healy? He was friends with a graduate student who developed schizophrenia. I had lunch with him in the student center to ask what I could do, who I could see. The next day Andy accused me of cheating on him with Dennis. He had been following me around."

Lara's expression hardened, and she balled up her fists on the table. Her gaze was accusatory, as if all this were the result of negligence on my part. I was no longer lost in reveries about our past. She was telling me that Andrew, the great Andrew on whom she had heaped such praise, had gone crazy. He had stalked her. I wondered what else he had done.

"I thought maybe Andy would get better, but he started sending me things I had thrown away in my garbage, and notes saying he was going to protect me from Horace Jacob Little. The 2D members voted him out of the house. I found him one night in my room. He said he was checking to make sure I was okay. For the first time I was really scared. There was this jumpy quality to his eyes I had never seen before. The Andy I had known was dead. This was a monster that had taken his place, stolen his memories and made them into delusions."

She removed a large manila envelope from her bag and placed it on the table.

"I avoided him for a while, but I knew how frightened and confused he was. So I forced him to go to the doctor and take his medication. It didn't make much difference. He didn't graduate. He moved to New York and I went back to Greenwich for the summer. I visited him once, to check if he was okay, but seeing him like that was too much to take. My parents convinced me I had to move on. I didn't hear from Andy anymore. Until yesterday. I got this in the mail."

She pushed the envelope toward me. Inside was a stack of paper barely held together by a flaccid rubber band—a manuscript of some sort. The title page read:

THE CONFESSIONS
OF ANDREW WALLACE

And the next page:

TO LARA,

THE MUSE OF MY LIFE

The rest of the pages, some fifty in all, represented the *Confessions*. The text was in a cramped and erratic handwriting, and on several sheets were stapled pages ripped out of a copy of *Strange Meeting*.

"It's his autobiography," Lara said. "Ever since Andy disappeared, I've tried to put him out of my mind. I'm working my ass off at NYU. I'm going out with Glen. The whole experience has made me a harder person. It's changed me. I want a pragmatic goal, and I'll work toward it. I'm done with romantic notions about love and life for a while."

I read the first lines of the autobiography, which struck me as irrational. I put the manuscript back in the envelope.

"I stayed up all night reading it, over and over again." She bit her lower lip and stared at the envelope. "I can't just turn my back on him, can I? The return address says Overlook Psychiatric Institute. I can't stand it, thinking he's hurt or locked up somewhere. What can I do? This is where I need your advice. I won't be upset if you want nothing to do with this. I felt you would understand somehow."

What if I had told her the logical thing? What if I had said, Lara, this guy is crazy and he's obviously put you through a lot, and you need to ignore him and get on with your life? Would everything that followed still have found a way of happening?

I admit to being thrilled that Lara had singled me out for "advice"—of all the people she knew at Princeton, of all the people she knew in New York. She could have discussed this with Glen, her boyfriend. Instead she was asking *me* for help, inviting me back into her life, saying she had been wrong to let our relationship end, wrong to have gone out with this guy who went crazy. This is what I heard her telling me: Help me end this horrible relationship with this lunatic, and maybe, just maybe, we can pick up where we left off. . . .

"I'll go visit him," I said. "I won't even mention that I know you. I'll tell him I'm writing an article about him for my newspaper."

Fogerty had been hounding me about my inability to generate good story ideas. "You want to be spoon-fed articles, like baby pap?" he would ask. "Jesus Christ, you went to Princeton! How about you put a little independent thought into this job?" In fact, he sent me off one afternoon to walk as far as I could up Broadway, with orders not to return to the office until I had found ten story ideas. Andrew's tale, dropped into my lap a few days after that misadventure, appeared to me in such a light. I wasn't sure I would really write an article about him, but it gave me a good excuse to see him.

"You don't think it's better to ignore him?"

"I'll see if he's okay. Then you can feel better about getting on with your life. Who knows? Maybe he's on some medication."

I unzipped my backpack and placed the *Confessions* inside for later reading. I told Lara I'd be in touch, and strode outside into the darkness, looking for a set of subway stairs.

cHapTer eIGHT

I spent that night reading Andrew Wallace's *Confessions*. I suppose the proper reaction would have been sympathy—here was someone with great promise who had been sidetracked into delusions and madness. But mostly I was intrigued by Andrew Wallace. His history was oddly bound up with mine. After Lara and I went our separate ways, he stepped in and took my place. Lara gave him the copy of *Strange Meeting* that I had given her. My interest in Horace Jacob Little was transmuted into his obsession. My actions and thoughts were reflected in him, distorted. I had played an unseen role in his life, and I wanted to meet him.

I called information and a mechanical voice gave me the number for the Overlook Psychiatric Institute, in Overlook, New York. After being bounced from one person to another, I was connected with a Dr. Saunders.

"I'd like to ask a few preliminary questions," I said. "Is Andrew considered dangerous?"

"None of our patients are dangerous, Mr. Burnett. Are you familiar with the nature of our community? We are an institution for the artistically gifted mentally ill. You might know us by our nickname—the Muse Asylum?"

I had never heard of anything like this.

"What was Andrew admitted for?"

"He voluntarily admitted himself after demolishing a car using a sledgehammer and his bare hands."

"That sounds dangerous enough," I said. "Does he have schizophrenia? Manic depression?"

"Andrew would have to give permission for me to talk to you about his case. And if you want to interview him, he'll have to agree. I will confer with him, and my secretary will call you with his answer."

Next I had to get Fogerty interested. He was initially unenthusiastic about the idea. It would involve the expense of renting a car and buying gas for the trip to Overlook, which was four hours north of the city.

"Why the hell should people care about this crazy kid?"

"People always care about crazy people," I said. "Isn't every other movie of the week about mental illness?"

Fogerty turned to his window and considered this. "Have you ever wondered what it would be like to be insane?"

"Not really."

"Imagine—every movement of the world would mean something special and secret to you. Delusions of reference, they call them. Every cloud, every birdcall would refer to you."

"I can interview him?"

"Does he *know* he's insane?

"I have no idea."

"I'm curious. If he really thinks there's a worldwide plot to kill him, does it ever occur to him he's imagining things? When the doctors tell him he's crazy, does he wonder whether they might be right?" Fogerty turned away from the window and faced me. "Why do you need to see this particular person? Why don't you pick a Manhattan lunatic?"

"I think I can work this into the story on Horace Jacob Little. Andrew Wallace is obsessed with Horace Jacob Little. He thinks he knows the secret of his identity."

This got Fogerty's attention. "What secret?"

"It's in this crazy autobiography he wrote. He thinks the original Horace Jacob Little was killed by someone who kept writing under that name."

Fogerty chewed on his pen, then laughed. "What an idea! The replacement of Horace Jacob Little by someone else. But what does that have to do with finding the author?"

"Nothing. It would make a great sidebar. I was thinking I could collect a bunch of screwball theories about Horace Jacob Little to offset our article about finding him."

Fogerty sighed and told me to save my receipts.

That afternoon I got a call from Dr. Saunders's secretary. Andrew was willing to talk to me.

THE NEXT DAY, I took the Triborough Bridge to the Deegan to the New York State Thruway toward Albany. As I pushed north and farther north, the traffic thinned and the landscape folded into steep hills that put my rented Toyota compact to the test. North. Local radio stations counted down the top twenty country songs. I did a hundred mph for a short stretch when I had the road to myself, and the car shook and shivered as though it would either take flight or come apart in its excitement. The white lines threw themselves under my wheels in desperate suicide. Sun streamed machine-gun fashion through the intermittent cover of leaves, small farmhouses and silos tucked themselves into the valleys, cows loitered near the hot roadside, hawks circled on updrafts, signs advertised "Mohawk Caves—Over 100 Chambers of Mystery." Optimistic blue stretched above and ahead where the road met the sky.

The town of Overlook was moderately famous as the home of a defunct chemical factory, once run by the D. G. Benderson company. In 1974, the town sank a new well east of the Benderson plant. By 1983, it had become obvious from the cases of leukemia in the north side of Overlook that the company had polluted the aquifer. Children died, and there was a civil court case, which ended in stalemate. Benderson closed the plant in 1987, leaving Overlook without its main source of employment.

The Benderson smokestack was visible from Main Street as I drove through town. The plant's closing had hit the place hard. I passed rows of houses sporting faded aluminum siding, their shutters leaning toward one another in conference over the state of things. Forlorn shopfronts held court on Main Street, surrounded by soaped-up windows and vacant parking spots. And every so often, the Benderson smokestack would peek through, a monument to cancer and decline.

OVERLOOK PSYCHIATRIC INSTITUTE differed so much from my expectations that I thought I had the wrong directions. I had anticipated an unremarkable hospital, something built in the utilitarian style of the sixties and mired in semi-neglect. Instead, Overlook resembled the country estate of a long-dead robber baron. Everything—the gate of ornate ironwork with spikes and bars that appeared to be in motion even before the guard opened it for me; the subsequent ten-minute drive through old-growth forest; the fountain spurting in the middle of the semicircular driveway; the mansion itself, of venerable granite weathered to slate gray, weeping with tendrils of ivy—bespoke great refinement, wealth and, paradoxically, total sanity.

I later learned that the mansion, which was on a hill overlooking the town, had originally been a residence of the Benderson family. A century ago, an artistically gifted member of that privileged clan came down with a severe case of "nerves." The house was given over to him and his doctor, who envisioned an artists' colony of sorts. The doctor invited other talented mental patients to live there, and the Muse Asylum was born.

I met Dr. Saunders after parking my car and entering the magnificent foyer, replete with a mural of turbulent Romans on the ceiling and gilt molding on the lofty walls.

The doctor was a stooped man with a pronounced limp, and was aided by a cane that opened at the bottom into a four-pronged claw to give a more secure purchase on the ground. Despite his handicap, he moved across the marble floor with surprising speed. Small brown spots showed through his thin white hair, and a close-cut white beard reminded me, as it might have been intended to, of Freud. He wore a dark suit and smartly shined shoes, and a handkerchief was folded neatly in the breast pocket of his jacket. I would not have been surprised if he had drawn forth a monocle to survey me.

"Mr. Burnett," he said, "Welcome to the Muse Asylum." He extended the hand unoccupied by the cane and stepped sideways, inviting me to walk farther into his domain. "We used to receive many requests from the press, but lately interest seems to have fallen off."

"Requests about Andrew Wallace?"

He smiled and put his hand on my shoulder, as if to comfort a neophyte with the assurance that everything would be explained in good time.

"No, Mr. Burnett. About our unique community."

DR. SAUNDERS TOOK me to his office, which was filled with snow-white busts, faded tapestries, copies of Pre-Raphaelite paintings, shelves burdened with decaying books, and dusty gray gargoyles. It was more like a storeroom in the British Museum than a doctor's office. He offered me a chair of dark, intricately carved wood that must have begun its life in a medieval monastery.

"Let me begin at the beginning," he said, pushing his fingers together in the shape of a tent and flexing them. "Overlook is a residence for the artistically gifted mentally ill. Two requirements must be met for a resident to be accepted: The patient in question must not be dangerous, and he or she must have demonstrable talent in the arts, whether that takes the form of painting, writing, or composing or performing music."

He paused as my scribbling pencil caught up with him.

"The patients are allowed to exhibit and sell their works, and the funds go toward the upkeep of the hospital. The main purpose of this community is to provide a therapeutic environment for the patients. We are a community here, Mr. Burnett. Patients feel comfortable with those around them and with the hospital itself, which as you can see resembles anything but a typically oppressive institution. In this supportive environment, art becomes the safety valve. Rage, repressed emotions and long-buried trauma all come tumbling onto the patients' canvases and pages. Disordered minds learn the discipline of technique—the control necessary for brushwork, the coherence required in narrative. In tandem with medications, we have been able to help a great many people. It is rare that someone leaves here less sane than he or she arrives."

"And Andrew is a writer?"

"That's right. He's hard at work on an autobiography now. Autobiography is usually the first assignment for our literary patients. We find it gives them a chance to examine their lives in such a way that the present moment seems the culmination of a lifelong journey—a good moment for change of a psychological nature. Furthermore, it introduces the idea that madness in works of literature must be harnessed and controlled. Autobiography forces the patients to write about their neuroses and delusions while imposing on them the structure of chronology. The hope is that this structure will positively influence the way Andrew views his own life. I think you'll see that Andrew has a real narrative gift. Now, Mr. Burnett, I would like to ask *you* a question."

I nodded and tapped my pencil on the notebook.

"How did you become interested in profiling Andrew?"

"He was in my class at Princeton. I heard through a mutual friend that he might make a good story."

"Years ago, we used to get scads of requests for interviews and profiles. You might want to look up some of those articles."

He glanced at his watch and asked if I had any further questions. If not, we would go upstairs to meet Andrew.

ANDREW WALLACE WAS lying on his bed, motionless and relaxed. He could have been sleeping, but I saw even from the doorway that his eyes were open and staring at the ceiling. He turned toward me.

"They are closing the walls on me, very slowly. If you stay still and watch, you can actually see the motion. This is a nutshell. Who are you? You look familiar."

He swung his legs off the side of the bed. I suppose I had vague expectations of straitjackets and frazzled hair and ranting and raving, or at least a sudden twitch in his cheek—some outward indication that his mind failed to control itself in the proper manner. He wore only a white T-shirt and those blue pants that doctors wear. The long hair he had at Princeton was gone, replaced by a streamlined crewcut. Without the ragged curls and tangles, he looked somewhat like me. We were hardly twins, and yet there was a rough symmetry in height, size, facial features. We might have been taken for cousins.

"My name is Jake. We were at Princeton together. I'm a reporter now and I want to write a profile of you."

A mixture of interest and terror passed quickly over his face, and he whispered, "Did he send you?"

"Nobody sent me. I'm a freelance reporter."

"How do I know you're telling the truth? How do I know he didn't send you?"

"You mean Horace Jacob Little?"

He narrowed his eyes and regarded me suspiciously. Whatever his appearance concealed, Andrew's voice and manner of speaking betrayed his illness. His words were laconic and flat. He seemed to lose interest in what he was saying by the time it left his lips. And then there were his eyes, flicking around the room, around my face, around my hands. They were dark and serious, in constant motion. He wanted to see everything around him at once.

"Why would Horace Jacob Little have sent me?" I said.

"Because he wants to kill me."

"Nobody knows who Horace Jacob Little is."

"He's using his influence to keep publishers from buying my book. My book—look."

Andrew rolled across the bed to the opposite side and reached underneath, fishing for and then retrieving a small strongbox, metallic green, with his name written on the top in permanent marker. He unlocked it with a key worn on a loop of string around his neck and removed four books, which I immediately recognized by their plain white jackets as works by Horace Jacob Little. He took out a sheaf of yellow lined paper with writing on it.

"This is my story," he said, waving the stack of paper. "And these are his. The paper is flammable and there are no working fire detectors in this hospital."

He offered me one of the Horace Jacob Little books and I looked through it. Every centimeter of white space was covered with Andrew's handwriting. He had filled the inside covers, the endpapers, the frontispiece, the blank outside covers, and then the margins of the text pages. Where there was room between the lines of text, Andrew's writing weaved itself among the printed words.

"I am engaged in a project to uncover the truth about Horace Jacob Little," he said. "Every word in his galactalogue is a potential clue. This is the only way for me to defend myself from him. I have to decipher his code and find out why he has arrayed his vast powers against me."

I saw I wouldn't get very far if I let on that I had already read the *Confessions*. Andrew would interpret this as more evidence that I had been sent to spy on him. I decided to play dumb.

"You have no idea why he's after you?"

"I know what he did to the first author, the ur–Horace Jacob Little."

"I didn't know there were two of them. What did he do?"

"There was only the name, the name and the words. There was no identity to weigh down the person. You see? To eliminate a person is difficult, but to kill an apparition, a collection of phrases, that's not hard. I imagine he tells himself he killed a ghost, not a person."

"So the current Horace Jacob Little is not the original author. That's why he's trying to kill you? Before you reveal his secret?"

Andrew took back the book. "I think Horace Jacob Little sent you to check up on my progress."

"Who do you think he is?"

"He's a voice that speaks without speaking. He is the story without the teller. He is the most obvious example of post–cold war espionage gone awry. He puts thoughts in my head and takes them out again. I don't really understand it."

"What if I just asked you a few questions?"

Andrew blinked several times in rapid succession. "No, no, no. If Horace Jacob Little did send you, I can't have anything to do with you. Even if he didn't send you and you print an article about me, he'll still read it and find out everything he wants to know."

I had to admit that this was sound reasoning, as far as it went. "What if I let you read the article before we print it. To check it for any secrets."

"Any story tells the secrets, even if you try to hide them."

Andrew was a former comp lit major, and that remark was worthy of his training. I walked to his window. The Benderson smokestack stood nearby like a prison tower. END RSON ran down the side in faded white type, spaces of dull brick where the elements had erased the letters. Andrew came and stood beside me, folding his arms to match my posture. We stared out at the town stretched below us.

"Do you know Lara Anne Knowles?" he asked.

"Sure. She was in our class."

"She's my fiancée."

"Really? Congratulations."

"She's going to be a lawyer. She's going to New York University School of Law. She means the world to me. I write to her every day. She has a hold on me from a previous life and she won't let me go."

I found this speech irritating. What upset me was my knowledge that I still wanted to be with Lara. The possibility that she might have reciprocal feelings was the underlying purpose of the trip to Overlook. Andrew's claiming Lara as his fiancée seemed only a little crazier than my own lingering desire.

"I'm dedicating my autobiography to Lara. Please do me a favor. Find Lara. Tell her I think about her all the time."

He picked up his manuscript again, suddenly animated. "If Horace Jacob Little doesn't prevent its publication, my *Confessions* may be the bombshell that finally blows his schemes wide open. If you really are a reporter and you don't work for Horace Jacob Little, then *that's* the story you should be working on. This is world-shaking, Pulitzer-winning stuff. Forget political corruption. This goes deeper."

I remembered Fogerty's question.

"When the doctors say you're mentally ill, do you believe them?"

"They're working for him, too. Why do you think he hasn't revealed his identity to the world? It doesn't take a mental patient to see that something is going on. I'm too tired to talk."

He picked up a sealed envelope from the windowsill. "I was about to send Lara another letter. I'm sure Horace Jacob Little is intercepting them. I had to bribe an orderly to smuggle out my *Confessions* and send it to her. Would you get this to her?"

I agreed, wondering whether I might be doing the wrong thing by humoring him. I wasn't going to get much more out of him, so I decided to let him know I had read the *Confessions*.

"'Strange Meeting' is one of my favorite Horace Jacob Little stories, too," I said.

He backed away from me and sat on his bed, watching me warily.

"I think this interview has gone far enough. You report back to your superiors and tell them they can go to hell."

He stretched out on the bed and turned away from me. As I left the room, the expedition to Overlook appeared foolish. I had driven all the way up there partly to satisfy my curiosity, and now that I had done so I was vaguely angry—perhaps with myself for trying to use Andrew as a subject for a news article (which now seemed a laughable idea), perhaps with Lara for getting involved with someone so clearly incapacitated, perhaps with life for sentencing someone from my class to that hospital and those delusions.

When I returned to Dr. Saunders's office, I found him sitting in front of his computer with his face close to the monitor, squinting as though unaccustomed to using the machine and doubtful of its continued cooperation.

"Come in, Mr. Burnett. Did you find your visit satisfactory?"

I asked him what the future held for Andrew.

"He should finish revisions of his autobiography within the next few weeks."

"Will he ever get better?"

"We're going to enroll him in a clinical trial of a new drug, Rydazine. We're guardedly optimistic. By the way, do you have a copy of his *Confessions*? Not for quotation in your article, of course. For background."

I didn't want to let him know that Andrew had smuggled out a copy, so I accepted the manuscript. I told him there probably wouldn't be any article in the end.

"That's a shame, Mr. Burnett. Andrew's is a fascinating story, and if he ever gets his act together, I think we can expect great things from him."

Dr. Saunders shook my hand and, as if this had been a visit not to an asylum but to a stately country home, insisted that I visit again in the near future.

CHapTer nine

FROM THE *CONFESSIONS* OF ANDREW WALLACE

I reach this juncture of the story and I hesitate to continue. I now stumble onto the secret that sets me at loggerheads with Horace Jacob Little, that forces him to try to destroy me. Here is the switch from light to darkness. Heretofore I was under the influence of a benign dispensation. At Princeton, I was more complete and happy than ever before. I woke up every day and looked at Lara, amazed that she could love someone like me (strange, impulsive, given to wandering off in the moonlight to contemplate the categorical imperative). Now everything changes. The rest of the actors walk offstage and leave me alone, in the darkness of the empty theater, where I continue the play in a valiant monologue to no one. Now the universe ceases expanding and, feeling its own weight, begins to collapse.

AN UNREMARKABLE SPRING day, senior year. The lawn outside McCosh Hall was soaked and muddy, scored by the solitary tracks of bicycles. I had not slept the previous night, for no good reason. Mysteriously, sleep was becoming unnecessary. I would climb into bed next to Lara and toss and turn, the wave of unconsciousness failing to break over me, my mind a bonfire of thoughts that would rage on and on. I would get up, read, listen to music, walk the deserted paths of campus until sunrise. I had lost one of the most basic human appetites, and in consequence I began to feel that the world itself was becoming a dream. I would attend a seminar and listen to people speaking, speaking, and it would seem to me that I had conjured the scene in my head and could make it disappear with a wish.

I entered McCosh, on my way to a lecture by Professor Mullin. I was not in the class, but he was speaking on Horace Jacob Little and it would have been foolish to miss a talk given by my thesis advisor on my thesis subject.

The crowd quieted as Mullin took the stage and grasped the lectern on both sides. I was seized by the conviction that the world around me was not real, that the scene was being projected onto a screen surrounding me. I was actually sitting in a dark room, strapped into a virtual reality machine. This was not an idle thought posited by my imagination. This was a terrifying idea that seemed undeniable. I had to restrain myself from poking in all directions to try to touch the screen. How can I convey my sense of disorientation? It was like being on a train in a station, told by your eyes that you are moving, only to realize it is a neighboring train that is in motion while you remain still.

I tried to pay attention to the lecture. I told myself I just needed sleep, which was true. Mullin talked about the relationship of Dante to the stories of *Strange Meeting*. He suggested that Horace Jacob Little was the perfect embodiment of postmodern theory, that he had almost been willed into existence by French intellectuals. There was a long digression about Wittgenstein. I became engrossed in the flow of the argument, thankful to be free of my odd episode of derealization. I took a few notes on points I wanted to discuss with Mullin.

A man rose from the back of the room and began to walk up the side aisle. He was dressed too warmly for the spring day, wearing a gray overcoat and a black watch cap. He also wore sunglasses, the kind a blind man might wear. I watched him make his way toward the stage. Mullin saw him but kept speaking. The man reached the stage and climbed the three stairs to stand on it. Mullin paused, stepped back from the lectern and regarded him.

—Can I help you? Mullin asked.

—You sure can. Let me say a few words.

Mullin tried to ignore him, but the man advanced on him. Mullin crossed to the other side of the stage and motioned to his graduate student. He leaned down to her and whispered in her ear. She turned and hurried out the door. Meanwhile, the man had reached the lectern. He tapped on the microphone with his fingers, eliciting a screech of feedback. He spoke in an urgent staccato:

—Hello, Princeton. I apologize for interrupting your class. Don't be alarmed or upset. You have been chosen to take part in an extraordinary event. People the world over have read the words of Horace Jacob Little, but how many people have seen him?

He stepped away from the lectern and raised his hands out to his sides.

—Behold the author. I am Horace Jacob Little. I am the Invisible Man, and I have chosen to make myself visible to you for one instant. My time is short. I am here to reveal to you the reason for my seclusion. The fact is, the Central Intelligence Agency is trying to kill me. You'd better believe it. I have the power to destroy the world. I know the secret of life. I have seen the condition of the soul after death. I have even received messages from our brothers in other regions of the universe. Oh, yes. You know what I'm saying. I don't have to spell it out for you. They think I'm dangerous and they are getting closer and closer to me. Yesterday I was taken to the United Nations building in New York and imprisoned. I managed to escape. I told one of the guards who I was, and he let me go. He was sympathetic to my cause. I'm here to tell you the truth. I'm here to reveal to you the world as it truly is. Everyone in this room has a sensor embedded in the brain. They put it there after birth. It allows you to be tracked, and it allows them to put thoughts in your mind. Mine is malfunctioning. It gives me too many ideas. That's why I'm an author. That's why they're after me—

By now the grad student had returned with four burly proctors in tow. The proctors mounted the stage. The man stopped raving and looked at them for a moment in silence. Then he shouted:

—The agents of darkness! The agents of darkness have come!

The proctors leaped on the man and wrestled him to the ground. The grunts from the struggle filled the stunned silence of the classroom. Handcuffs appeared and were applied. The man unleashed toward the rafters a stream of profanity, curses and yelps. The proctors led him out of the lecture hall, his eyes wild with madness.

For the rest of the class, for the rest of the day, I could not stop thinking, What if that really *was* Horace Jacob Little? Who says Horace Jacob Little couldn't be crazy? And if that wasn't him, then who was? Who was? Who was?

THE NEXT DAY, I took this matter to Professor Mullin himself. He fixed me a cup of tea in his office and drummed his fingers on his desk. He said:

—The interesting thing about that incident is how it points up the problems of anonymity. What credence do we give to a text of unknown origin? Could it have been written by a madman? Anything is possible.

—So you think I'm right? That could have been the real Horace Jacob Little?

—Anyone could. You, me, the secretary in the department office.

He winked at me, absurdly, in the manner of one who wishes to signal another surreptitiously. He was trying to tell me something. He continued, in a low, conspiratorial voice:

—I mean, how do we even know there has been only *one* Horace Jacob Little?

My heart was accelerating, my mind waking, my awareness doubling, tripling. I understood that Mullin was not simply relating a "theory." I had lived my life for the purpose of hearing his words. They penetrated to the center of my being, where they resonated and refused to leave.

—How many Horace Jacob Littles have there been? I asked.

—I'm just making that up, of course.

He winked again, to make sure I understood.

I DESCENDED TO my carrel in Firestone Library, where I had gathered virtually every book by or about Horace Jacob Little. I was alone in the dark recesses of C-floor among acres of dusty, unread books when I understood for the first time.

"Strange Meeting" tells of the replacement of Seamus Small by an identical twin. The twin usurps the place of his victim and lives on in his stead. The world is unaware of the switch. I had already determined that "Seamus Small" was a clever code for "Jacob Little," meaning that the author had written the story about himself. I assumed the story had to do with the drastic change in artistic vision that occurs in that book.

But when Mullin told me Horace Jacob Little might not be just one person, everything became clear. "Strange Meeting" was a confession of a real-life murder. Horace Jacob Little had been killed and replaced by another. The world, which did not know the identity of Horace Jacob Little, was never the wiser.

Where were these ideas coming from? Not from my own mind. I was not constructing this as a logical argument, internally generated and subject to revision and rejection. Instead, some benign spirit was sitting next to me, pointing to the books and whispering the true meanings. I remember looking at my hands and finding them shaking uncontrollably. I wanted to see more, to know more, to never come to the end of these connections. If only I could spend the rest of my life in that library, I would find the connections among all the books, all the ideas they contained. If only I could keep listening to my spirit guide, the voice beside me that was now louder and impossible to ignore . . .

I EXPLAINED MY idea to Lara.

—Look at it this way, I said. With the publication of *Strange Meeting*, Horace Jacob Little's writing style undergoes a total change, right? From modernist to postmodern overnight. What's the most logical explanation for this? That he went to a writing workshop and retooled his prose style and worldview? No. The most logical explanation is that someone rubbed out the original author, the first Horace Jacob Little, and continued to write in his name.

To my surprise, Lara began to cry.

—Stop, she said. I never want you to think about Horace Jacob Little again. You haven't been thinking about anything *but* him for weeks. Look at yourself. I mean it. Take a step back and look at what's been going on. You haven't done any schoolwork for weeks. You've been turning this room into a pigsty. When was the last time you combed your hair? What the hell is wrong with you?

—Nothing's wrong with me. I finally understand what's been going on under the surface, that's all.

She looked at me, tears streaming down her perfect face. I would have done anything to make her happy, so I said I would stop, even though I knew I was powerless to prevent the thoughts from coming.

—Please, she said. Just please.

PROFESSOR MULLIN WAS away for a week at the Modern Literature Consortium conference, held that year in Des Moines, so I wrote him the first of what would become many letters on the subject.

Professor Mullin:

I want to thank you for taking me into your confidence in this matter. I am happy to report that your faith in me has not gone unrewarded, as I have thought long and hard about the information you conveyed, and I now comprehend the true import of the Horace Jacob Little situation. I suppose we should meet soon to discuss the best avenue for making this public. Perhaps a news release would be best. Or maybe we should simply go to the police and let them in on the secret. (Although I realize even as I write the previous sentence that the police would never believe us. Or maybe they wouldn't care. Or even worse, they might already be on Horace Jacob Little's payroll, in which case our going public would place us in danger.) No more by mail! One never knows what prying eyes might find, and of course the "snails have ears" too. We must meet in private to discuss this further. Until the greening, as they say, I remain,

                                        Yours in the Word,
                                        A.W.

chapter ten

The computer at the *Ledger* that I commandeered for searching the Web looked like it could navigate a nuclear submarine. It comprised a case of shadow-black plastic, smoky gray keys, blinking pale green lights, and an oversized monitor intended for viewing the layouts of pages of newsprint. Surrounding the seductive machine in comical contrast was the perpetual mess of the *Ledger* office—discarded drafts, mutilated envelopes, coffee stains on the fraying mousepad.

One of the first things I found relating to Horace Jacob Little was an excerpt of an article he had supposedly written on the expansion of cyberspace. It preached the end of the novel and the advent of hypertext, with which a reader could click his or her way through a story in any order. Horace Jacob Little connected this with the influence of Roland Barthes, who proclaimed the death of the author and the liberation of the reader from the tyranny of plot.

"The 'novel' of the future will quite literally have no form other than electronic," Horace Jacob Little wrote, "no plot other than the multiplicity of possibility, and no author other than the reader. Barthes's death of the author will be an accomplished fact."

Even as I read and imagined him saying the words in the deep voice I thought of him as having, I knew I couldn't trust the authenticity of the article. Anyone could have set up a Web page of his own rantings and signed Horace Jacob Little's name to it. When the author remains hidden, all kinds of unusual business can be done in his name. Then again, maybe Horace Jacob Little really *had* written the article. This confusion was apparently what he wanted to create. If the author is dead, everyone can write in his name. It only made me more interested in tracking him down so I could ask him about it.

I also found a note posted by a Columbia student who had been reading *Strange Meeting* on the subway. A bearded man approached him and asked whether he liked the book. The man proceeded to quote long passages by heart and to explain the symbolism and the ideas behind several of the stories. The student concluded: "His demeanor was that of a subway preacher. He was overbearing, assertive, comfortable in the knowledge that he was on the path of righteousness. His text was *Strange Meeting*, not Revelation. There is of course no way to verify my suspicion, but given the stranger's familiarity with the book and his refusal to tell me his name, it seems likely that he was none other than Horace Jacob Little himself."

Horace Jacob Little was rumored on other Web pages to be researching his next novel in Budapest, traveling incognito with a band of Gypsies. He was said to be living in a remote international scientific outpost in the Antarctic. He was reported to have bought a small island off Costa Rica and declared himself dictator. One Web page gave an extensive excerpt of what was supposedly his upcoming novel about the life of Shakespeare, told in the first person. There was no way to tell whether any or all of this was apocryphal. Horace Jacob Little seemed less an actual person than a myth handed down from generation to generation, a bogeyman in a tale that varied wildly with the teller.

I wasted a week wandering in the wilderness of the Internet. I found myself in all manner of places. Professors had posted scholarly papers on his texts. Connoisseurs of psychedelic drugs had set up a discussion group to speculate about what substances Horace Jacob Little most likely used. Some people thought he was responsible for a string of mail bombings in Texas. Hundreds of photos had been posted, all bearing the caption "Horace Jacob Little," and no one of them similar to any other. A man in Ontario claimed he was Horace Jacob Little's illegitimate son. A stripper in Memphis offered a free private show to anyone who could prove he was Horace Jacob Little.

I wondered whether I was as crazy as these people, all of us madly believing in what might not exist. Horace Jacob Little was only a curiosity to them, something unusual and seemingly contrary to the natural order of things—the bearded lady in the carnival, the Invisible Novelist.

My undirected trips through the Web were getting me nowhere. I was going in circles, as all the pages were interconnected and cross-referenced to one another. I was lost in the woods and stumbling onto the same clearings again and again. I needed the help of an expert.

I ARRIVED AT the building housing George Faber's brokerage firm at the time he had specified when I called him for assistance—nine in the evening. The soaring marble lobby was deserted except for a security guard behind the control desk, listening to a Yankees game. He let me pass without a word, absorbed by the fate of a long fly ball. I went up to the fifty-third floor and found my way into a darkened office space, vacant for the night, a warren of cubicles made eerie by the glow of scattered emergency lights. I saw a figure walking at the other end of the room, across the labyrinth. I hurried down an aisle to intercept him. He was a barefoot man in his twenties, dressed in shorts and drinking from a can of Coke.

"I'm looking for George Faber," I said.

"I was hoping you were the pizza guy," he replied. "George is down thataway."

As I walked down the hall I passed a dozen small offices, each of which contained a youngish employee staring glassy-eyed at a computer screen. In an office at the end of the hall I found George, slumped over his desk, asleep with his mouth open. I shook him.

"Oh, God," he said, waking with a start and rubbing his neck. The knot of his tie was three inches below his neck, hanging from a rumpled shirt. "What time is it?"

"I can come back if now is bad."

"No. I just finished a big project. I was catching up on some sleep."

"You usually stay this late?"

"Actually, I've been here a few days. It's not a big deal. There's a futon downstairs, and a kitchen, and a bathroom with a shower."

"Are you kidding me? Why?"

George yawned and shook a Coke can on his desk to see if there was anything left.

"You know," he said, "just because you decided to tune out or drop out or whatever you call it, doesn't mean the rest of us are excused from working."

"Hey, I'm working. I need your help with a story I'm doing."

"The reclusive author."

"Horace Jacob Little."

"What a touching story. Two old roommates reunite to strip an innocent citizen of his right to privacy. This could be a movie of the week."

George had always been sarcastic and gruff, especially when he thought humans didn't measure up to the rigorous standard of logic set by computers.

"You don't have to help," I said. "I've been looking on Web pages all week—"

George interrupted, shaking his head. "The Web isn't going to help you with this. All you'll find is a bunch of fan pages set up by lunatics. If he's remained anonymous this long, he must be really careful. Tell me again why this is important."

"Horace Jacob Little is one of the most influential authors of our time. I don't want to run a big tabloid exposé. I want to interview him about his ideas, his sources of inspiration, his philosophy of life. I think he owes that to us."

"Don't you think he's already put into his books whatever profound things he has to say? I'm only an ex–computer science major, but this obsession with finding him doesn't make much sense."

George was the only person besides Fogerty who knew about my search. I wondered whether people would agree with him.

"Shakespeare scholars pore over every possible source for clues about his life, right?" I said. "He's dead—logically speaking, who cares about the details? But people care. They have his signature in the British Museum and people go to see it like it's God's own handwriting."

"Well, I don't care about Shakespeare or Horace Jacob Little. I'll tell you why I'm willing to find him. Hacking has become idiotic. What's the fun of breaking into some stupid dot-com? Anyone can do it. This is different. No one has ever found Horace Jacob Little. This is new. This takes talent."

He was already devising a strategy, just as he had when playing Martian Slaughter. He cupped his hand over his mouth and turned to his computer, earnest and businesslike. George brought a fierce devotion to everything he set his mind to, whether killing computerized aliens, analyzing stocks or locating reclusive authors. I envied him for it. Had he been in my place he would have gotten a job at the *Times* and taken it as his goal to have an article above the fold on page one.

"I think it can be done," he said. "We need a network that has some information about him."

"The Department of Motor Vehicles?"

George shook his head dismissively. He was deep in thought and unconcerned about civility. "No, that's no good. He probably doesn't have a license, or else it's under a different name. That's an obvious place, and I'm sure people have looked there already. Same with the passport agency and the IRS. What we need is something less official, like an e-mail archive. Who would Horace Jacob Little send e-mail to?"

We both thought for a moment.

"His agent," I offered.

"Who's that?"

"No one knows."

George stood and walked to his window, which looked out onto the lights of innumerable buildings below and in the distance. The city stretched to the limit of the horizon below a pall of ghostly clouds. A plane floated in the dark, blinking complacently, as it descended toward La Guardia.

"How about his publisher?" I said. "Lucent Press."

"That's a possibility. But they would be very careful about this kind of thing. Anyone deeply involved in Horace's life or work would be too smart to leave a trail. We need someone who happened to have a fleeting contact with Horace and dropped him an e-mail. Someone who didn't know enough to be careful."

My train of thought moved through varied terrain. I tried to come up with an organization Horace Jacob Little had occasional interaction with. Gusts of wind roared against George's window and shook the building perceptibly.

"*The New Yorker*," I said. "He publishes a story there about once a year."

George nodded, slowly at first and then more vigorously.

"Okay. Step one is to get into another network and use that location to get into the *New Yorker* server."

I realized what George was envisioning. "This is illegal, right?" I said.

"No, Mr. Journalist. This is investigative reporting."

I WAS NOW out of the hunt. George began typing commands meaningless to me and receiving equally cryptic replies. He stared at the computer screen with such intensity that he seemed to be employing a form of telepathy. He would whisper to himself sporadically, running his hand over his chin. He tried to keep me updated, but his bulletins involved too many acronyms. I soon gave up trying to stay abreast of our progress.

I wandered over to his window and looked at the city from the fifty-third floor. The sky was lit with a diffuse glow from the millions of individual lights. I watched cars moving in slow motion up First Avenue. I looked across the East River, toward Queens and the general neighborhood of my apartment. I thought to myself, Horace Jacob Little could be anywhere out there, anywhere. Wind continued to buffet the building, making a soft moaning sound. I was disconnected from the world below. George and I were conducting our search from the vantage of a satellite.

Near twelve o'clock George was still going strong, fueled by an infusion of black coffee and sugar-coated doughnuts I procured from an all-night deli across the street.

"There's no need to finish this now," I said. "We can pick it up tomorrow morning."

George would hear none of it. "Take a nap if you want. You can't just stop in the middle of something like this."

I curled up on the floor in a corner of his office. When I woke it was three in the morning and I felt as if the curve of my spine had been permanently altered. While I was still in the fog between sleep and waking, George began to talk about another party he was planning, at which I grunted, and about the guests he wanted to invite, at which I grunted, and about Lara and Glen, at which I did not grunt.

"Can you believe how good she looked?" George said. "I mean, she was always incredible, but now she's on a different level."

"She's dating an asshole," I said.

"Glen Thaler? Yeah, she could do better. Considering what she's been through, I think she's happy."

"What? You mean Andrew Wallace going crazy?"

"You mean you don't know about—" He stopped working at the computer and stared at me.

"What?" I was growing hot, my stomach tightening.

He wheeled his chair closer and leaned his head toward me. I was still on the floor, but now I was sitting up straight. He lowered his voice to an excited whisper, even though no one else could conceivably have been listening.

"I'll tell you how I found out about the whole thing. I was in a Shakespeare class with Lara spring semester senior year. We're reading

Hamlet in the class, doing the scene where Polonius sends, what's her name, Ophelia to talk to Hamlet. All of a sudden Lara bolts out of the class. Then a few weeks after graduation, she was at home. Apparently her parents had heard all about Andrew and forbade her to see him, which they were probably right to do. She swallowed a bunch of pills. They had to take her to the hospital and pump her stomach. She was admitted for about a week."

"I had no idea." I couldn't sit still. I got up and paced the room, picking up and examining the objects on George's desk. The Swingline stapler, the starcruiser paperweight.

"After I heard about Andrew," he said, "I put it all together. Ophelia is in love with Hamlet, and he goes insane, taunting her, mocking her."

"I can't believe I didn't hear about this."

"You were in Europe at the time, right? Then Minneapolis? That's what you get for being out of the loop. I didn't see her afterward until the night of my party. That's why I was surprised she looked so good and normal."

Lara's trying to kill herself was the debasement of something sacred, the desecration of an icon. This new knowledge had the power to change my fundamental outlook on life. It would darken my world like a sky painted by El Greco, brooding over a forsaken town. I didn't know how far things had gone. I was helpless to stop myself from imagining the scenes: Her mother finding her limp and cold. The crowd of people standing outside her mother's house as she was carried out on the stretcher. Lara staring blankly out her hospital window as a shrink asked her about suicidal ideation. I hated the fact that I hadn't known about it, that I hadn't kept better tabs on her. It had become a point of pride not to keep track of her. But I had failed her in some way.

I tried to justify it, to comprehend an action that the Lara I used to know would have been incapable of. She arrives at Princeton young and naive, the product of a sheltered upbringing in a sheltered town. She has a fling with me and watches her parents get divorced from across an ocean. She returns, angry, rebellious, looking for something new, and latches on to 2D and Andrew Wallace. When Andrew loses it, she's left with nothing. Lara's behavior at George's party seemed odd to me because it *was* odd. It was a rejection of her past, an attempt to start over on more favorable terms with life. I could hear it in her voice that night, an insistent and self-delusional undercurrent beneath the smile and the beauty: Everything's fine, I'm okay, Life is leading to somewhere wondrous and worthwhile. . . .

"Remember how happy she was back in the Monastery," I said. "Before all this happened."

"You mean when you went out with her."

"When I went out with her."

I would never have expected from George—the gruff, logical guy with only the most basic appreciation of human emotion—the look of sympathy or the softness in his voice as he said, "Stay out of her business. I'm telling you as your friend and hers. She's had a rough time with Andrew. Now she's on stable ground again with Glen. You don't like him? Too bad. Leave her alone."

ONCE WE HAD gained access to the *New Yorker* files, we searched the e-mail archive for the name Horace Jacob Little. We found no matches. We tried "Horace," which yielded hundreds of e-mails to and from various Horaces, including one employee who appeared to be obsessed with conspiracy theories about the Kennedy assassination. Trying to avoid missives about the failings of the Warren Report, we came across the following e-mail:

X-Authentication-Warning: jasper.newyorker.org: jlfulton
owned process doing-bs
DATE: Fri, 3 Apr 1998 04:19:20-0600 (EST)
FROM: "Javier Fulton" <jlfulton@jasper.newyorker.org>
SENDER: jlfulton@jasper.newyorker.org
TO: "Abraham S. Gilner" <asgilnero2@quasar.com>
SUBJECT: Re: "Universal Language"
Mime-Version: 1.0

Horace,

The story is fantastic. Unfortunately, there was some
confusion about the final graph:

> As Jack wanders the city he sometimes pauses beneath
> the great shimmering glass-and-steel skin of a skyscraper,
> waiting for it to come apart above and around him. He sits
> before his TV switching among an endless montage of
> things unrelated—the new-model Range Rover, yester-
> day's assault on the Kurds, Bubble Barbie, planes appeared
> to violate the no-fly zone, the cockroach is older than all
> mammals—until they become related. He wonders how
> long we can last, how long before everything is shattered,
> our tongues confused, our purpose made several. The
> coming destruction is visible to him, but there can never
> be an end to A Universal Language. The conclusion will
> remain a solitary knowledge, unspeakable.

What does this mean? Has Jack lost his mind? Is he only
imagining that what he writes about is coming true? Is his
writing partner performing the acts of terrorism? These are

all questions I am left with, and this rather vague paragraph does not do enough to answer them.

I'll be in touch about other edits.

—Javier

"That's a story Horace Jacob Little published last January," I said, slapping George on the shoulder. " 'A Universal Language.' It's about a novelist who has writer's block and teams up with another author to write a novel about terrorists called *A Universal Language*. Then some of the bombings they write about actually start to happen."

George didn't care about the story. "Look at the e-mail address. Abraham S. Gilner at Quasar.com. That's the name Horace has on his e-mail account."

He proceeded to break into the subscriber database of Quasar. com, an Internet provider, and search for the billing address of Abraham S. Gilner. It was on the Upper West Side. I had expected Horace Jacob Little to be hiding at the ends of the earth, not within my jurisdiction as a reporter. Maybe Abraham S. Gilner was paying his bills for him. Or maybe that was Horace Jacob Little's real name, or a pseudonym. I was ecstatic, now feeling more certain that it was going to work, that I was going to find my literary hero and write a brilliant article.

"You're a genius," I told George. "I can't believe it."

He stood and stretched, then bowed in a fatigued and triumphant motion, the way a conductor might slump after a torrid performance. I told him I owed him dinner or something.

He waved his hand. "This was fun," he said, sitting down. "I've been so busy with work that I haven't done much hacking lately. Just promise me no one will ever know I was involved in this."

"No way. I promise."

I gathered my things to leave. George remained at his desk, staring.

"Aren't you coming?" I asked.

"No, I think I'll stay here."

"The futon downstairs?"

"If no one is on it yet."

George looked exhausted. I felt sorry for him. He should have been starting an Internet company and having fun, making a fast million on stock options, not slaving away for a brokerage house. Had he really chosen to go into this line of work, or had he done what his parents had expected from him at the end of college?

I remembered him as he was when we roomed together in the Monastery. "Jake! Jake!" He would shout while he clicked away at his computer. "Check it out! I found the headquarters of the Galactic Overlords in the Vega system." He would perform operations that allowed him to send forged e-mails to people around campus, causing some memorable chaos. And now here he was, settling into the machinery of Wall Street. He might someday be among its principal cogs. He had Picassos on the wall of his magnificent loft, which he apparently visited only on occasion. And there on his desk was a miniature model of a starcruiser, a memento from times when he moved at the speed of light.

"You know," he said as I was leaving, "nobody's going to be reading novels fifty years from now. It's a dying art, like opera. People will look back on Horace Jacob Little as quaint and esoteric."

He was playing devil's advocate, trying to rile me. I wasn't sure he was wrong, but I didn't care about the future of the novel. That was too abstract, like worrying about when the sun will explode. I had a more concrete concern, and now a concrete address.

I LEFT THE building with that invaluable address scrawled in my notebook. I was surprised to see the sky already brightening over the deserted and silent streets. In my sleepy delirium, I decided to go immediately to the Upper West Side and continue the search. It was important not to pause. A pause would squander the inertia George and I had generated. I boarded an empty uptown subway and took a seat.

I woke up on the elevated tracks of the Bronx as the train rocketed around a curve. I had missed the Upper West Side. The car was now full of early-morning commuters and the sun streamed through dirty windows, catching and revealing graffiti etched in the glass. ZEUS, SANE, LORAX, WES2. The mysterious names of the underground, made luminous by the light of day.

CHAPTER ELEVEN

The address listed by Quasar.com was just off Central Park West at the northern end of the park. Some blocks south, townhouses and brownstones ran in the seven figures, but the block I walked on in search of Horace Jacob Little was too dingy to be trendy or expensive. The building I found, although technically a townhouse, had little in common with its cousins downtown. It was gritty, plain-fronted, plastered in a uniform gray and connected to identical neighbors. Soviet architects might have admired it.

At first I thought of simply buzzing upstairs and offering a pretext to ask for Abraham Gilner, assuming that this name would lead one way or another to the author. But I regarded Horace Jacob Little much as a bird-watcher might consider a rare and skittish species. One sudden movement and the fabulous creature would be gone, a flutter of red wings unfurled in flight. The frustration was maddening, far worse than it had been when I was potentially continents away from my goal. We were so close that I could communicate by means of a loud bullhorn, and yet he remained a featureless blank.

I retreated across Central Park West and into the park itself, placing myself among the trees and bushes. I had a good view of the building across the street, and I waited. There was a sign nearby that warned "Rodenticide" above a graphic of a menacing rat. I watched where I stepped, not sure whether to be concerned more about the rats or the poison.

Finding myself with time to ponder such things, I attempted to identify the poison. Was it a pill? A powder? I poked the twigs and underbrush with the toe of my shoe. I found only bottle caps and coffee stirrers amid the pale brown Manhattan earth. I watched the traffic streaming up and down Central Park West, racing taxis and sedate minivans, jalopies and imports. The July heat made the blacktop shimmer. Every sequence of the lights brought the cars to an identical halt. An identical mini-gridlock developed as excess traffic spilled over into the intersection. Identical curses were yelled and fingers extended. A time-lapse videocamera would have illustrated something like what I saw as the hours passed—the melding of those vehicles into one mass, one wave of motion, one superheated tentacle of metal and taillights stretching the length of Manhattan.

An elderly woman emerged from the door of Gilner's building and proceeded down the stairs. She had a shopping bag on one wrist, and a leash attached to a small white poodle on the other. As she descended she gripped the railing with both hands and gingerly placed both feet on each step. I considered that Horace Jacob Little might be a woman. I watched her plod down the street. After half a block the dog, which had been running along in front of her atop a blur of tiny legs, stopped and defecated. The woman removed a wad of tissues from her bag and cleaned up the mess, then deposited it in a nearby trashcan. As she passed from sight I entertained the image of her seated before a typewriter, placidly composing, secure in the knowledge that she was the last person on earth who might be suspected of being Horace Jacob Little.

Soon a man appeared in the doorway of the building. He wore faded jeans and a white dress shirt. He was tall and powerful-looking, with a torso packed with pounds of sinews, a frame that lifted his head above those of other mortals, and gray hair that came almost to his shoulders. His bushy white beard fluttered in the breeze like a windsock. It was a beard worthy of Tolstoy or Whitman or some other bearded master. I once read that when drawing a caricature, the cartoonist must select one feature of the subject to exaggerate outrageously. A caricaturist would undoubtedly have focused on this man's beard. It was tremendous, the color of an overcast sky, so central to his appearance and demeanor that he would have ceased to exist without it. I had also read that according to Hebrew scripture, Nazirites were consecrated to God and prohibited from cutting their hair or shaving their beard, from which they drew power and strength. The man would have made a fine Nazirite. Once I beheld him and recognized that he could be Horace Jacob Little, all other possibilities were instantly eliminated. Here was a perfect case of the vocalist's matching the voice.

I thought of simply approaching him and snapping pictures from right in front of him, like a paparazzo. But when I considered the size of the man, I realized that he might bludgeon me with his tremendous fists before ripping the film from the camera and moving someplace where he could never again be found.

I followed him westward, trying to stay a good distance behind. I experienced the thrill the criminal must feel, totally absorbed by the crime, heart pounding with audible intensity, every nerve ending at the ready for the arrival of the next crucial stimulus.

Horace Jacob Little's image had never, as far as the world knew, graced the lens of a camera, or photographic film, or the inverted universe of the negative. After I identified him, there occurred a flurry of picture-taking that must have made up for all those years of invisibility. I wanted the perfect shot of him—alone, in good light, looking my way. Fogerty was under the impression that we would simply run a picture or two of Horace Jacob Little, along with a short explanatory note about how we had found him. I had too much respect for Horace Jacob Little and his quest for anonymity to let that happen. I had my own plan.

As I followed him from his apartment, I took the first picture, using the enormous telephoto lens that Phil, the photo guy at the *Ledger*, had given me with the admonition that he would kill himself (rather than me) if I broke it.

Number 1: The back of Horace Jacob Little, waiting for the light to turn at Amsterdam. The first picture a stranger had knowingly taken of the man.

I trailed him downtown to the big West Side Barnes & Noble. He spent the afternoon and into the evening reading in the store's overstuffed armchairs. He began, appropriately enough, in the fiction section, picking his own books off the shelf and absently paging through them. He seemed to be checking paragraphs at random for their accuracy. Before moving on, he took out a gold pen and signed one of the books.

As soon as he walked away I raced over and examined the signed book. It was *Strange Meeting.* His signature sprawled across the title page in royal blue ink, decorative and stylish. Just above it, he had marked through the printed version of his name.

When I again caught sight of him, he was in the medical section reading a book about the human brain. The way he reclined in his armchair, stretched almost to his impressive full length, made me suspect that he spent a lot of time there. I stopped a passing clerk and asked if the man with the beard was a regular customer.

"I can't tell you that," she said, glaring, and walked off.

In the history section he read parts of a biography of Andrew Jackson. In the poetry section he read Yeats and Wallace Stevens. In the sociology section he read about shopping malls. All the while I was snapping pictures from across the store, the distance shrunk magically by that admirable lens. It was dark by the time Horace Jacob Little left the store and walked back to his apartment. I had become used to following him, and I was no longer worried he would notice me. Our movements were synchronized. Our strides matched. Our turns and courses were symmetrical.

When I left him, I had four rolls of exposed film and a signed copy of *Strange Meeting* in my book bag.

ON THE SECOND day of my stakeout I followed Horace Jacob Little to Broadway. He jogged down a set of subway station stairs and headed to the turnstiles. He passed a Metrocard through the reader. A mechanism malfunctioned with a loud clack and froze the metal arm in the half-closed position as he tried to push forward. Without hesitation Horace Jacob Little placed his hands on the neighboring supports and swung himself over the turnstile like a pole-vaulter.

The station was so narrow that the tunnel barely swelled where it met the platform. Given the close space and the periodic arrival of subway cars screeching and hissing in their eagerness to hit someone, most people tended toward the middle of the platform and stayed put. Horace

Jacob Little, however, roamed at a fast pace, treading on the perilous edge of the platform when the middle was too congested. His meandering seemed pointless and, as I attempted to follow, somewhat dangerous. Photographs were impossible—the light was too dim and the crowd too dense. I also worried that someone would steal Phil's beloved lens if I wielded it too brazenly.

On the subway, too, Horace Jacob Little exhibited an inability to stay still. He walked from car to car, purposefully, as though he had left a personal item in the back of the train and was determined to retrieve before it disappeared. As the train swerved and turned in the darkness, I fought for my balance, grabbing poles, swinging straps, sometimes gripping shoulders. Where was he going? When he reached the final car he would exit at the next station, wait for the following train and again begin his journey through the cars. He seemed to be looking for someone who had told him only, Meet me somewhere on the Broadway local, sometime in the afternoon.

This went on for quite a while, and I grew accustomed to the chase, the uncertain balance, the roar between cars that made me imagine a screaming animal racing through its underground den. The progression from car to car became repetitive, and my mind wandered, so much so that I almost passed Horace Jacob Little on what must have been our twentieth train. He had stopped his chase and taken a seat in a moderately crowded car. He removed a small reporter's-style notebook from his blazer and began scribbling furiously with his gold pen. He glanced furtively at an elderly woman sitting across from him. His eyes darted back and forth from notebook to woman. I would have guessed he was drawing her picture had I not seen he was writing. Was this the person he was looking for? She didn't appear to know him.

Horace Jacob Little rose, went through several successive cars and sat down to give a middle-aged man in a dirty fedora a similar treatment. I realized he was making character sketches. He had been looking for a face that was radiant with an untold story.

I was not going to take any photographs on the train, and there was no telling how long Horace Jacob Little would keep up this expedition. I followed him through a few more trains and let him lose me between Canal and Franklin.

ON THE THIRD day, under an auspicious but unforgiving sun, I followed Horace Jacob Little to a coffee shop on upper Broadway. After meditating on the man for weeks, rereading his books, searching for him, and then watching and following his every public movement, I found it remarkable that he still had no idea who I was. In the fluorescent light of the coffee shop, under the faded sign giving directions for the rescue of choking victims, I felt it was time to make introductions.

I sat down in a booth catercorner to his and began reading *Strange Meeting* with the cover splayed and vertical, hoping he would be unable to resist commenting on some aspect of the stories.

Halfway through my sandwich I was interrupted by his voice. It was soft and insistent, with an undercurrent of whisper that demanded immediate intimacy.

"Hey, man. Which story are you reading?"

" 'The Lord of Close Vicinity.' "

In that story, an old Spanish priest named Sagredo discusses the return of Columbus from the New World. Father Sagredo is troubled by reports that humans were found inhabiting the new lands. Realizing that the Bible cannot account for the presence of these peoples, he seeks out the king and begs him to cover up the news of the voyage. The king refuses, and Sagredo predicts that mankind will look back on his decision as "the first moment of the end of the world."

"Did you know," Horace Jacob Little said, "that 'Lord of Close Vicinity' is a translation of *Tloque-Nahuaque,* the name of an Aztec deity?"

I lowered the book slowly, pretending to be suspicious.

"Are you a Horace Jacob Little fan?"

"A big one," he said, nodding. "Hey, why do you think he picked that name for a story about the hypothetical beginning of disillusionment with the Western religious tradition?"

I felt like a professor had called on me in class. "The Aztec god is a forgotten deity, with no power other than that due to the fact people once worshipped him. They used to appease him with human sacrifice."

"And now the Christian God is the same way? That's a good theory."

"Is that the point? The story doesn't gloat about the loss of religious certainty. It's more an elegy. Is Horace Jacob Little really a secular humanist?"

He glanced up from his food and stared at me warily, as if suddenly wondering whether he had gone too far. "I don't know," he mumbled. "Maybe you should ask him."

"Maybe I should. Maybe I just did."

I got up and slid into his booth, facing him. He started to signal for the check.

"Before you go," I whispered, "I need to discuss something with you."

"Waitress."

"There's no need to hurry."

He swiveled his head, searching for the waitress. He looked bes-
tial, with his long gray hair flying and his eyes dilated in apparent
fear and rage.

"Look at this," I said.

I pushed a picture of him across the table. It was taken in the
Barnes & Noble history section. He was looking straight at the camera. The picture quieted him at once. He examined it with undis-
guised hatred, holding it close to his face and pursing his dry lips.

"What do you want? Money?"

I turned around to make sure no one was listening. The only
other occupants of the place were an elderly man and his hyperactive
granddaughter, both seated across the room.

"I'm a reporter. My editor gave me the assignment to find you,
and I did. But here's the thing. I'm also a huge fan. All this time I've
been looking for you, not because I want to expose your identity, but
because I want to talk to you."

Horace Jacob Little was unmoved by my revelation. "What do
you want?"

"If you agree to give me an interview that I can publish, I'll give
you the negatives to all the pictures."

"What makes you think I care? I can disappear overnight to anywhere in the world."

"Do you know how many Web pages would have a photo spread
of you by the end of the week? You'll spend the rest of your life on
the run."

He stared at me defiantly, before crumpling the photo in his fist
and dropping it on the table.

"I really hate doing this to you," I said.

"But you want to know more about me. That's infantile. Really childish. Why should you have to know me to read and enjoy what I write?"

"Look at what you just told me. 'Lord of Close Vicinity' is the name of a forgotten Aztec god. It changes everything."

"Go to hell."

"Mr. Little. I—"

"Go to hell!"

The man and his granddaughter were staring. I stood and delivered a brief speech I had prepared.

"Genius demands recognition, Mr. Little. I admire your writing immensely. I admire you. I don't want to run the picture. I don't want people to recognize you on the street. I do want people to know your philosophy, your ideals, your sources of inspiration. I want to know these things, too."

He rose from the table without a word and exited the restaurant, leaving me to pick up his check. I had bought Horace Jacob Little lunch.

chapter twelve

Professor Mullin spoke earnestly to me about psychological counseling. He said I was extrapolating and bringing into being baseless theories. He told me about doctors at the campus health center. I kept writing him letters, longer letters, not just about Horace Jacob Little but about other things, whatever crossed my mind. It all fit together somehow, I was sure of that. My words to him were a way of trying to explain my new world to myself.

Who else could I tell, for example, when I noticed that I was being followed around campus? I would see people posing as students, wearing the crispest college fashions, riding pristine bikes. In the morning I would see a blond man in a red windbreaker. I would also see him across the street in the evening. This happened far too often to be mere coincidence. I began keeping a notebook in which I recorded the movements of these shadows. I waved and yelled at them to let them know I was onto them.

It was impossible to finish any schoolwork under that sort of pressure. Mullin insisted that I talk to the counselors at the health center. Otherwise I might fail my thesis, he said—as if failure in academic work were of any concern to me, when my personal safety was threatened each and every day.

Mysteriously, Mullin began to ignore me. When I passed him on campus paths he would turn in the other direction, check his watch, do anything to avoid engaging me in conversation. I understood that I had displeased him. One day I saw him in the bookstore and he gazed on me with pity, not apathy. He was fighting back tears as he stared at me. He had apparently learned something about my life that made him feel sorry for me. I knew it had to do with Lara.

I was losing Lara.

I thought she would have been eager to share with me the adventure of uncovering the truth of Horace Jacob Little's identity. Instead, she refused to let me speak of it.

—You're not yourself anymore, she would say.

—Who am I?

—Just go talk to the doctor, for God's sake. Will you do that? For me?

—There's nothing wrong with me. Nothing at all.

What was it that Mullin had pitied me for? Had he discovered that Lara was being unfaithful to me? I resolved to find out.

IT IS REMARKABLY easy to track someone across the Princeton campus. Shaggy trees, small alcoves in the battlemented walls, and scattered sculptures abound, all suitable for concealment. And of course the place is flooded with students, to the extent that when classes are released it is impossible to walk in front of McCosh Hall without dodging streaking bicycles, groups of political scientists and hurrying math majors. Lara had no idea I was following her. For seven days I did nothing else. No classes. No homework. Hardly even any food. A constant vigil to discover the terrible secret that Mullin's expression had hinted at.

I also tried to access Lara's records in the dean's office, but I wasn't able to pick the lock to West College. I barely escaped from a proctor who saw me trying for the fourth time.

During that week Lara had lunch at the student center with someone else. Three times. I had never met him, but I located him in the facebook. This person was Dennis Healy, from Tenafly, New Jersey. I sat unobserved in a darkened corner, munching cheese fries and realizing that this was the person Mullin had known about. It was clear now. Lara had fallen for Dennis Healy, and Mullin's far-flung network of spies and remote listening devices had picked up the signs. It was this network that allowed Mullin to discover the truth about Horace Jacob Little. Mullin had grown close to me over the course of the year, but he was unwilling or unable to reveal the existence of his sources, so he slyly communicated the truth about Horace Jacob Little's replacement. Similarly, his look of pity had been a hint about Lara's infidelity. He hoped I would have the brains to put two and two together.

Well, I did. And I found Dennis Healy, sucking chocolate milk through a straw and looking flirtatiously at Lara. He was a disgusting specimen—flat head, slovenly dress, two-day beard. She was bantering with him, crossing and uncrossing her legs. I wanted to march over to their table with a length of cord and wrap it around Dennis Healy's throat. He would gasp for breath and wave his arms comically before I let him go, to recover his life and wait in dread for the next time I struck.

ONE NIGHT, I decided to tell her that I knew.

—We need to talk. I see what's going on.

—What do you mean?

—I mean you and this Dennis.

She pretended for a moment to be puzzled.

—You mean Dennis Healy?

I forgave her. Her infidelity didn't matter at all. I wanted to tell her that she had hurt me, and that I would be watching her to make sure she was always safe from Horace Jacob Little.

—I've seen you and him having lunch together—very intimate, the two of you. And I've heard you calling him at night. You two have quite a code worked out. Professor Mullin tipped me off to the situation. How long did you think this could go on without my knowing?

—What the hell are you talking about?

—You know damn well what I'm talking about!

I wanted to get out of there before I lost the control that was steadily escaping me. At the same time, I knew that when I left I would be leaving our love behind forever.

—Don't worry, I said. I'll watch over you. You'll always be safe. There are dangerous people out there—conspiracies and secret societies most people would never even dream could exist. I think these people are interested in me. If you ever realize how much you love me, or how much I love you, just say the word and I'll find you.

I left in a hurry, physically and emotionally exhausted, a different person from the one who had entered the room. A valve had been released in my psyche. I could feel the electrical impulses surging down new neural pathways. I wandered the campus for several hours, thinking only about Lara's eternally kissable mouth and my banishment from that eternity.

SOON AFTER THIS they voted me out of the 2D house. I had no say in the matter. The housing office moved me into a spare single room at the Grad College. At night when I wandered the campus I would meditate on my new world. All was confusion. By this time I had realized there was a vast conspiracy behind the Horace Jacob Little replacement. How else to explain the people following me? I thought a great deal about the author and his plans for me. I also thought about Lara. Only weeks before, I had been together with her, blissfully happy. As inexorably and as decisively as the seasons change, my life had been transformed. I was alone in the world once again, facing an enemy I did not understand. I wanted so much just to hear her voice, to hear her tell me everything would be okay. Some nights I could think of nothing to do but lie on the grass in Prospect Garden, surrounded by the sweet scent of the nocturnal buds, staring up at the black sky.

One night I went by the 2D house and poked through the trash outside. I soon located Lara's garbage. I found nothing particularly interesting at first, only the usual tissues, broken pencils, drafts of papers, the shell of a vanished deodorant stick. At the bottom of the bin I found a picture she had taken of me one day when we skipped class and went to New York. It had once hung at the top of her mirror, fastened with transparent tape.

In the picture I was on a bench, smiling, with the skyline of Central Park West visible in the background. Lara said she liked the picture because it looked as if I were at the center of the city. She said:

—All those buildings are your dominion. You're surveying your kingdom from the throne.

It was a superb summary of my life at the time. When I was with Lara it was easy to believe that I was at the center of things, that the buildings were sentient beings nodding in silent approval of our happiness.

In my dreams I often return to that day in New York. We went all over the city, riding the Number 7 train into the ethnic neighborhoods of Queens, the el rusting and peeling over streets that were a chaos of unknown words and Chinese characters. Lara priced saris in Flushing under the curious eyes of the Indian women around her. I asked myself, Why not stay here? Why not forget about Princeton and get an apartment here in Queens? I would take a menial job, and Lara and I would live together in bliss. At that moment, with the citizens of the world rushing around us in a babel of languages, all happiness seemed to depend on our love. The fate of the world was tied up with the rightness of my hand on the small of her back.

I wrote her a letter, which soon became one of dozens. She didn't want to see me, but there was nothing to stop me from wooing her via the written word.

Lara—

I am enclosing this picture, which accidentally fell into the garbage. I know you don't want to lose this memento of our relationship. Do you remember that day? The glorious clatter of the el, our quiet walk through Central Park, shopping for saris in Flushing . . . But those are just memories now, for me to treasure and hope that someday they can be repeated.

Please don't be alarmed if you see me following you around campus every now and then. I have learned that there is a plot involving several professors. I do not yet know the goal of this plot. I have reason to believe that they are watching the both of us. Don't worry. I will protect you from anything and everything. I will do this because I love you.

Andy

P.S. Why don't you put the picture back on the mirror? You said it looked like I was at the center of the city. I was. I was.

The low point came when I saw Lara walking across campus with Professor Mullin. I tried to follow them close enough to hear their conversation, but all I caught were occasional words. Nevertheless, I heard my name several times. They were talking about me. That was when I understood that Mullin was not on my side in this matter. I had assumed from the beginning that he and I were allied against Horace Jacob Little, that together we would bring the truth to light. Now I saw another possibility. He was working for Horace Jacob Little. Why else had he been so unresponsive to my letters and overtures? Here he was discussing me with Lara. *He* had turned her against me. What better way to destroy me than to poison my love? I was overwhelmed by a rage I had never before experienced. My enemies were stronger and more organized than I had thought. They were dismantling my life, piece by piece.

I crossed the Rubicon. Either I would win completely, reveal Horace Jacob Little's secret and win Lara back, or I would be utterly destroyed in the process.

That night I confronted the person following me, a young woman in a Princeton baseball hat. I had seen her trailing me several times over the course of a few weeks.

—You can tell your boss I'm not going to take this lying down, I shouted.

She tried to turn and walk the other way, acting confused. I wouldn't let her go. I was livid.

—This can't go on. You tell that motherfucking author I'm through playing games.

CHAPTER THIRTEEN

Since starting at the *Ledger*, I had gone a few times after work to the Brooklyn Heights promenade, which is separated from downtown Manhattan by only a thin channel of river. Being there is like floating in a rowboat about to be plowed under by the oil tanker of Manhattan, towering above and blowing its numberless horns.

In the solitude beside that somber river, as the reflected buildings shimmered in the black water, I would consider my situation. I was more than a year out of college and still unsure what I wanted out of life. The *Ledger* was not a bad job, and I was enjoying the search for Horace Jacob Little, but journalism in general struck me as tedious and mind-numbing. I thought about enrolling in graduate school but made no firm resolutions.

There were always other people on the promenade when I was there. They were lovers, cooing and cuddling on the benches. Or they were bald men worried about their jobs, young women recently divorced, strangers alienated from whatever they had once hoped to belong to. We walked and circled and watched the skyline, finding in it the possibility that the rest of the city was actually as small as we were.

I told Lara to meet me on the promenade one brutally humid night in July, just after I had found Horace Jacob Little. I did not tell her about the letter Andrew Wallace had given me for her.

I had been there for some time, watching daylight drain from overhead and night advance from Brooklyn toward the skyline, when she arrived. She wore a white tank top and a skirt that almost swept the ground. When she drew close I could see her skin was moist and glowing in the heat of the summer night.

"Okay. I was skeptical," she said, looking at the buildings of Manhattan. "Dragging me out to God knows where in Brooklyn. But this is impressive."

We were silent, listening to the muted roar of the city around us. It sounded like a distant waterfall in a deep forest.

"I live over there, around NYU." She raised her arm and indicated a space across the river where the buildings shrank and the city dived to the earth, thinking better of the vaulting ambition it displayed farther downtown and uptown. "Andy once told me why there are no tall buildings there. It has to do with the bedrock. In the middle of the island it goes too deep to build a huge foundation on. The life of a city predetermined by geology."

"I didn't know he was a geologist, too."

I could tell she was nervous about receiving my report on Andrew's condition. She twined together her thin fingers as they rested on the railing.

"I used to tease him by asking obscure questions. You know, 'Oh, well if you're so smart, why don't you tell me about the economics of precolonial Polynesia.' The great thing was that sometimes he would be interested in the question, and he'd spend a day in Firestone doing research on it instead of going to class. He'd say, 'By the way, remember what you asked about the Tonga people? They have this amazing social structure.' "

She paused and seemed to be searching the East River for signs of the Tonga, perhaps a flotilla of canoes in the falling darkness. She was more comfortable talking in general terms about how wonderful Andrew used to be, rather than getting into the specifics of the inferior present.

"The world was a playground for him," she said. "That's what I miss. I mean, look at me now. I go to class, I study, I watch TV. But Andy made me feel there were no limits to what I could know and do. We used to talk about taking a trip around the world after graduation. That's probably what I would be doing right now. . . ."

She let her voice trail off, then asked, "How is he?"

"He thought Horace Jacob Little sent me to check up on him. He thinks you're his fiancée. He's confused. He speaks in wild bursts. I didn't know him before, so I can't really say if he's worse or better."

"No, he's worse. He's worse. When we first started going out he wasn't crazy at all. He was just . . ." She searched for the appropriate word for several seconds before giving up. "He was just Andy. You must be completely baffled by the fact that we went out."

"It's crossed my mind that it's a little weird."

"I was attracted to him because he was so different. But all that stuff he wrote in the *Confessions* about multiple souls and alternative universes—that's all new. I'll catch a few accurate glimpses of him in the *Confessions,* but for the most part it's like Andy in a fun-house mirror. Was it obsessive to spend full days in Firestone reading about obscure topics just because they interested him? Maybe, maybe not.

Then he stepped in front of the curvy mirror and it bent everything out of proportion. He lost access to some signal that told him which ideas were crazy and which weren't."

I removed the letter from my pocket and handed it to Lara. She knew immediately what it was, and opened the envelope without speaking. She unfolded the letter and began to read.

"Even his handwriting is different," she said at length, and put the letter in her bag.

"Doesn't he send you letters?"

"No. Only that packet with the *Confessions.*"

"He says he writes to you every day."

"The hospital must intercept them," she said softly with her eyes closed. "All I want to know is, is Andy happy? I have horrible dreams about *One Flew over the Cuckoo's Nest.*"

"No, it's not like that. Do you know what Overlook is?"

"A psychiatric hospital," she said.

"It turns out to be a place for the artistic mentally ill. They have a house full of painters and musicians and writers. They call it the Muse Asylum."

Lara looked at me like I was making this up.

"I'm serious. That manuscript he sent you is an autobiography they're having him write. He wants to be a writer."

"And it's a nice place?"

"My God. You should see it. It's an old mansion that used to belong to the Benderson family. I think all the original furnishings are still there. Andy has his own room on the second floor. The patients pretty much have the run of the place."

She smiled, for the first time that night. A ringing erupted from within her small black shoulder bag. She extracted a cell phone and excused herself to answer it, tossing her hair as she brought the phone to her ear.

"Oh, hi . . . No, I'm in Brooklyn. . . . With Jake, that friend of mine . . . I could probably see your building, but I'm not sure which one it is. . . . I can't really talk now. . . . What time? . . . Okay. See you."

She hung up and returned the slender phone to the bag. "Glen," she said.

"How did you two meet?"

"He's the son of some friends of my parents. We actually went to preschool together in Greenwich."

"Your parents set you up?"

"Well, sort of. They've always joked that he and I would get together and fall in love. Glen's parents and mine go way back."

"So they were right all along."

Lara shrugged. "Glen's a great guy. . . ." Then, as if aware of the territory she had stumbled on: "It's too hot. Let's get out of here."

THE NEW *LEDGER* was out, and I wanted to get a copy to see if my latest article had come out all right. I hopped on a Manhattan-bound train along with Lara. We stood, gripping the same pole, craning our necks to read the advertisements. We puzzled out the translation of a Spanish ad for a chiropractor. We read about the scourges of AIDS, asthma, systemic lupus erythematosus, drugs and domestic violence. We sped through the night, stopping intermittently, watching in the dark window our twins floating outside the train, ghosting us.

A strange thing began to happen. All at once Lara threw off her dark mood. We did not talk about Andrew. We pretended he didn't exist, pretended he had no claim over our thoughts or memories. Lara let her hand fall over mine on the pole. In my mind, years were erased. We were freshmen again, on our way from the dining hall to the Monastery through a night of soft breezes and purple clouds. And helplessly, my soul surged as she smiled at me and swayed with the motion of the train, so close.

We exited the subway and ascended into the hot night of the Village. Cabs and buses and private cars jostled for space around Union Square, lurching to stops and starts, their horns like the cries of penned animals. The lights of buildings and stores and megastores twinkled in the humid air, an exquisite backdrop conceived by God for an opera of unknown length and beauty. For the first time since I had moved to New York, I saw the city not simply as an encumbrance to be borne with, or as the source of the perverse and violent acts that were subjects for my articles. It was the raw material of my new life. I had dreamed during my youth in Minneapolis of walking down busy streets such as this, on hot summer nights such as this, with a beautiful girl such as Lara, who was now talking excitedly and walking quickly, as if some long-awaited joy lay waiting around the next corner, or the next.

We located a *Ledger* box on a corner near her building. I flipped through the paper and found my article on page six. It concerned a home-care nurse who had bilked her elderly patient out of hundreds of thousands of dollars. I'd had fun writing it. I had gone to the building where the patient lived and talked to a doorman who told me the nurse started showing up for work in a chauffeured limousine.

Lara was thrilled by my byline. "This is like when you used to write for the *Prince*. I'd pick up the paper every morning and think, What did Jake write about today?"

"You did that?"

"Until you quit."

After reading the first few paragraphs of the article, she said, "Let me ask you something. When did you become such a cynic?"

I had been focused on Lara's problems. It never crossed my mind that I might appear changed to her. "What do you mean?"

"You were always such an idealist. Your columns in the *Prince* burned with self-righteousness. I thought you were going to be a great writer, at *The New York Times* or something. You seem to just be drifting along."

"I am," I said. "I'm waiting for God to strike me from my horse and reveal to me the way to salvation."

"That's a perfect example of what I'm talking about. You say that with irony, but I think deep down that's what you're really hoping for. You're still a romantic idealist at heart."

Lara's little analysis took me by surprise. We never feel that others are scrutinizing us with the same attention and diligence with which we scrutinize them. I could only shrug and agree with her, happy to have become in her eyes a person worthy of such investigation. I was about to return the favor and let her in on what I had gleaned about her psyche, but I knew she probably wouldn't find the results flattering, so I kept silent.

A song escaped the open door of a bar, along with the din of nightly rituals. I remembered the song as one of Lara's favorites from freshman year. She grabbed my hand and stopped me, and sang a few bars in a sweet voice as we stood there, the city rushing around us through the kinetic night.

WHEN WE REACHED Lara's building she did not hesitate to lean in close to kiss me good night on the cheek, intending a peck. In a fluid motion I slipped my arm around her warm body. She stayed still for a moment, and I could feel her breath on my face. She lingered, her lips in the vicinity of mine, waiting, saying amazing things with her eyes and wet lashes.

After we kissed she stepped back and looked at me, not breathing. Without a word, she turned and walked into her building. Her eyes told me to follow her.

We breezed past the security guard and took an elevator that was waiting. On the ride up she remained silent, staring at the electronic floor indicator with a furrowed brow. In her dorm room, I grabbed her around the waist even before the door had a chance to slam shut. She leaned her body into mine and we kissed, sloppily, desperately. I could feel the heat coming off her breasts, her face, her legs. I slipped my hands under her tank top and ran my fingers over her smooth skin, slick with sweat. We were almost struggling against each other, breathing quickly, pushing each other into and away from the wall.

"I missed you," I said, when my lips were momentarily free. I instantly regretted saying it. The words seemed to stun her. She stared at me as if waking from a dream.

"I can't do this." She broke away into the dark room. When she switched on a light near the couch, I saw that she was angry.

"Is that what this whole thing is to you?" she said.

"What? What thing?"

"This is all another opportunity for you to get in my pants?"

I should have excused myself, saying there had been a misunderstanding. I should have told her I would call the following day to figure everything out. If she was angry, I was furious. All the emotion that had been drawn up and abandoned—lust, love, joy, whatever you want to call it—now turned to anger. I moved toward her, yelling.

"No, that's Glen's job," I said, drenching his name with as much contempt as I could muster. "And let me tell you what I think. I think the way you've been acting is ridiculous. Showing up at George's party like everything is fantastic in your life and then moping around the rest of the time thinking about Andrew. Sending old friends to check up on him. If you had even a shred of feeling for Andrew, you would go visit him yourself. Or do you just forget about people when they no longer meet your approval?"

This was untrue. I didn't blame her for not visiting Andrew. I only wanted to fling words at her that would sting as much as the ones she had said to me.

"Get out," she said. "Go. Leave." She looked like she was about to cry.

I couldn't bring myself to leave. I regretted every word I had said. Lara fled down a short hallway to her bathroom and closed the door. I could hear a few sobs, which tore through me. Everything was going wrong.

I heard running water, and she emerged with her face red and damp, her eyes shining. I stood stock still, lest a movement on my part be interpreted by her as a sign of base intent.

"Don't you know I would do anything if Andy could get better?"

My mind was processing information at an astounding pace. We were dealing with an accumulation of emotions that were not limited to love or longing, but included a backlog of regret and nostalgia and resentment. Did I really want Lara, or did I want the memory of her, the emblem of some irretrievable innocence? I thought of Andrew Wallace, standing at the window, telling me that Lara was his fiancée.

As I watched her struggling to control herself, on the verge of surrendering to an emotion from which she could not recover, I truly grasped the extent of Lara's feelings for the old Andrew. I crossed the room and stood before her. Almost resignedly, she leaned forward and put her head on my shoulder. I understood I would never win her back, and that Glen had never won her. It was Andrew, and she was lost.

ON THE WAY out I met Glen in the lobby. I saw the recognition flash across his face.

"Jake, right?"

We shook hands. My expression must have held a clue of what had taken place upstairs, because he asked suspiciously what I was doing there.

"I was talking to Lara about Andrew Wallace," I said. Glen returned only a blank stare.

"Who?"

"I think she had better be the one to tell you," I said, and left him by the elevator.

She had never even told him about Andrew. This struck me as the saddest thing I had learned over the course of the wrecked evening. So great was her desire to outdistance her past that she had decided to keep that swath of it a secret, to make of Andrew a revenant only she could see. Until I came along and started to bring him back to life.

chapter fourteen

The day of the big interview, Horace Jacob Little was waiting for me, blocking the open doorway to his apartment. His tufted eyebrows were a single glowering strip across his forehead, supporting the trenches of angry wrinkles above. It was clear that since our last conversation he had not been reconciled to the idea of an interview.

"I thought of having you arrested for harassment when you showed up. But I want to keep the pictures out of the paper. You have the negatives?"

"First the interview."

He shook his head before standing to one side and allowing me to enter.

The apartment was several rooms on the top floor of the townhouse. The ceiling sloped toward the sides of the room I entered, and I gathered that the space used to be an attic. A pair of small dormer

windows threw diffuse light into the gloom. He had no air condi-
tioner, and all the summer heat of the building had risen to his sti-
fling garret. Books were everywhere. Three walls were hidden by
shelves sagging under their dusty load. Books sat on tables and chairs
in piles that reached to three or four feet, and were strewn about the
floor, making my progress into the room difficult. Crumpled and torn
sheets of paper littered the floor in the gaps between these obstacles.

The fourth wall was hung with what appeared at first glance to
be wallpaper of an irregular pattern. In fact, it was an arrangement of
hundreds of sheets of paper, each covered in typed paragraphs and
messy handwriting. Red arrows traveled from page to page, some
stretching the length of the wall. Beneath this wall was a table covered with a gray wool blanket.

"Don't look at that," he snapped. "I said you could interview me,
not inspect my apartment."

Horace Jacob Little sat on his couch, pointing me to an adjacent
chair. I moved a stack of books to the floor and sat down. I took out
my notebook and a tape recorder.

"Is that how you write?" I pointed to the sheets on the wall.

"Actually, I'm plotting strategies for Scrabble."

He smiled oddly. It was not a friendly smile. He looked like he
was entertaining a fantasy of strangling me but was nevertheless
smiling to be polite.

"Let's begin," I said, pushing the Record button and placing the
tape recorder between us on the arm of the couch. "You are considered by many to be the greatest living American novelist. Why do you
feel it's necessary to remain in hiding?"

Horace Jacob Little stared at the tape recorder for what seemed
an eternity.

"I listen for my muse, and I can only hear her in silence. Writing is an intensely private process. I'm afraid there's no grand philosophical justification for my secrecy. The desire to know all about an author is a sign of laziness on the part of the reader. It's easier to digest a work of literature when you can attach it to a face, or a set of political beliefs or life-style choices. When all you have is the text, or a body of work, you have to confront what is written."

"Tell me about your childhood."

Horace Jacob Little threw his hands up. "This is ridiculous. A very poor excuse for an interview. You come in here asking crypto-Freudian questions about my childhood, as if that could explain anything?"

I paused the tape recorder and said, in as matter-of-fact a tone as I could muster, "If you refuse to participate in this interview and answer my questions, I'll walk out of here and we'll run the pictures."

He stopped breathing and his face became crimson. Mastering his emotion, he swallowed hard and blinked. I switched the tape recorder back on and asked another question.

"Perhaps the biggest mystery surrounding your work is the distinct shift in tone that occurred in 1987's *Strange Meeting*. Before that collection, you tended to write about love and emotional struggle, but in that book and after, you gravitate toward madness, surreal environments and intellectual puzzles. What prompted that change?"

"So now you think you have arrived at the heart of the matter? You detect an eddy in the lifeblood of the artist? Well, if you look at certain early works you can see a clear interest in the matters I focus on in *Strange Meeting*. But having said that, I think I did evolve as a writer. If I wrote the same thing over and over again, I wouldn't be satisfied, and I don't think my readers would be, either. It happens that in 1986 someone gave me a copy of *Ficciones* and, even though I had read Borges when he was first translated into English, I was captivated anew by the stories. Both consciously and unconsciously, *Strange Meeting* was the result of an effort to take my writing in new directions. I've always thought that the best writers are like ventriloquists, changing voices and tones when appropriate."

"So what's your real voice?"

"The one I'm using now."

"Do you consider yourself a postmodern writer?"

"A very crude term, and therefore a meaningless question. You must have been trained at some god-awful university. Is your next question about my opinion of Derrida? Shall we discuss the futility of using language as a means of communication?"

I sat silently, waiting for an answer. I was expecting wisdom, compassion and generosity of spirit, not mockery and scorn. Now I saw the possibility that the creative process was married to a handicap in the mind of this creator—a misanthropy that drove him away from the rest of us, or made us drive him away.

"Come here," he said, rising. "I want to show you something."

I took the tape recorder and followed him across the room to the table covered by the blanket. He whisked it off, revealing a diorama of a field filled with rows and columns of miniature soldiers dressed in seventeenth-century uniform. He picked up one of the soldiers and handed it to me.

"This is a hobby of mine. I buy the metal figures and paint them. I can spend hours on a single soldier, intent on getting every detail right, even the shine on the boot buckle. Then I set them up on the table. What you see on the wall over there is my next novel, spread out for editing. I'm doing the same thing with my characters that I do with the soldiers. If you can get the details right, down to the boot buckle, then the world you create can have something to say about the world we inhabit. All the rest, all the critical terminology, amounts to navel-gazing in pursuit of tenure."

He placed the soldier back on the field, adjusting its angle of attack until it was perfect.

"I've always found the term 'postmodern writer' distasteful and vague. Dickens used multiple and sometimes conflicting narrative voices in *Bleak House.* Conrad was writing about alienation and absurdity at the turn of the century. Wells was writing about the collision of technology and society during the same period. These are supposedly postmodern concerns, but they belong to a much wider range of authors. Forster said that all the great authors should be thought of as sitting together in the Reading Room of the British Museum, rather than separated into different centuries and movements. That's a much better way to think about literature than this absurd pigeonholing so common among small minds."

From underneath the table he removed a package wrapped in plastic, which he then opened. He unwrapped an underlying swaddle of cloth, to reveal an antique handgun. The barrel was longer than that of a modern pistol, and the handle was a beautifully carved block of wood, bearing in its center the circular insignia of a charging buffalo.

"Do you like my gun? A valuable antique, 1871. It still works, though."

He put the gun to my head and whispered in my ear, so close I could almost feel his tongue: "If you don't keep your end of the bargain, if you run the pictures, I will track you down. The police won't find me—no one knows who I am."

"If anything happens to me, they'll run the pictures," I said, my voice sounding quite small.

He replaced the gun in its cloth covering. "Let's move this along, shall we," he said, nudging me toward the couch. I could feel the power of his body. The pressure of his hand made me miss a step. He did not need a weapon to pose a credible threat.

I calculated that I could be out of the apartment within two or three seconds should the need arise. I considered turning off the tape recorder and walking away, but to do so would have been to admit a grave mistake. I couldn't run away scared from the man I had idolized. I forged ahead when he sat down again.

"Since this is the first interview you have ever granted, I think I would be remiss if I did not give you the opportunity to discuss specific works. I'll begin with *The Unreal City*, your first novel, about a woman torn between her family life and a developing attachment to a cultic Christian sect. What prompted you to write it?"

"I won't discuss my early work."

"Why not?"

"Next question."

"What are you working on now?"

"I would never reveal it before it's done. Remember, I'm the author obsessed with privacy. But I'll tell you a little secret, off the record. The novel's about a reporter who tracks down a reclusive author, mercilessly exposes him to the public and . . . well, I haven't gotten to the conclusion yet. I call it *The Shadow Knows*."

He laughed, a deep chortle that went on for too long. He was enjoying himself now that he had seized control of the interview. All I could do was continue to ask questions.

"Critics have suggested that the 'web of society' in 'The History of London' has special relevance, given that you have removed yourself from society. Was this in your mind when you wrote it?"

"I identified with the figure of the antiquarian because both of us are either constructing or reconstructing lives while holding ourselves apart from the world we live in. In the end, the antiquarian finds himself caught in the web woven by his own society and he becomes just like one of the characters he has written about. I feel that to write, I must remain distant and observe from afar."

"How do you spend an average day?"

"This is ludicrous. Why should people care how I spend my days? I'm not a movie star. I don't parade myself around like a celebrity. Why can't I have a few shreds of privacy? If you must know, I'm the most boring person in the world. I read for much of the time. I'll wander the city looking for inspiration or story ideas. And then I stay up late at night writing. It's a simple, almost monastic life that I'm sure will disappoint everyone who believed I was dogsledding to the North Pole in my spare time."

Abruptly he stood and said, "Okay—interview's over."

When I started to protest, he said, "You don't want to get me upset."

I had enough to write an interesting article, though not the soul-searching dialogue I had hoped for. I turned off the tape recorder.

"Give me your wallet," he said.

"Why?"

"I want to see your driver's license."

I did as he said. He reached for a pen and paper.

"Okay, Jacob Burnett, I'm copying your address and ID number. I expect to see those negatives by this time tomorrow. And I'm telling you, if the story runs with pictures or incriminating details, I will hold you personally responsible." These last words he emphasized by jabbing his forefinger forcefully into my chest. I was about to go, when he blocked the doorway.

"One more thing."

He took a sticker from his pocket and peeled it from its backing.

It was one of those name tags people wear at business conventions: "Hello! My name is . . ." Horace Jacob Little had written his name on the tag, and he affixed it to his shirt.

"This is what you want, isn't it? Now I'm ready to meet my public." He erupted into laughter. Appalled and unsettled, I made my exit, leaving him roaring with glee.

ONCE OUTSIDE AND around the corner, I slumped against a wall and massaged my temples. I was exhausted by the interview and almost sick with disappointment. I had met Horace Jacob Little, the man who was to take me under his wing and reveal to me his noble philosophy. He turned out to be a pompous, eccentric brute in a messy apartment who had no better answers to the important questions than I did. I wanted to go home and forget the whole thing ever happened. I needed to spit out the memory like a poison. But a line had been crossed, a taboo broken, and I sensed that the excruciating interview would become a seminal event in my life.

Back at the *Ledger* office, I told Fogerty the interview had not gone well.

"Who cares?" he said. "We're selling the fact that we found him, not his actual answers."

"I thought I was doing a great thing by getting him to speak. I thought researchers for generations would look back on this article as a key document for Horace Jacob Little studies."

"Listen, they will anyway. This is a hell of a coup. It's going to be big news."

"We need to send him the negatives and the prints."

He gave me an odd look, as if trying to figure the best way to tell me something.

"What?" I asked.

"In this business, you learn to cover your ass. We'll send the negatives and a set of prints. But we'll keep another set of prints. We won't run them, but we should have them just in case."

I wondered what type of ammunition a gun from 1871 would shoot, and whether it was available in the city of New York.

THE ARTICLE APPEARED in the July 20 issue of the *Ledger*. I did not include in my article the part about the gun, or the threats, or the business with the name tag. I simply reported in general terms how I had found him. I described the layout and decor of his apartment, and provided a transcript of our brief discussion. The article occupied less than half a page of newsprint. Fogerty, true to his word, did not run the pictures.

When the article appeared, it caused a small sensation. The Associated Press and Reuters picked it up the next day. *The New York Times* and most of the other big papers ran articles about the emergence of Horace Jacob Little. I heard the words I had recorded and typed used as sound bites on CNN and in national news broadcasts. I had not realized so many people cared about Horace Jacob Little. Maybe they began to care only once he had been found, when they had tangible evidence to latch on to.

The *Ledger* was inundated with calls from other news organizations, literary agents, publishers and the book-buying public. Fogerty marched around the place like a general who had won a war against fantastic odds. It was all a mistake. Horace Jacob Little was infiltrating the culture around me—his words beamed on electromagnetic waves, sent over e-mail, read over cellular phones. Before the interview, such attention would have struck me as appropriate. Now it seemed misguided.

OTHER REPORTING DUTIES supervened, and the following day I went down to One Police Plaza for an article I was writing on police brutality. When I returned to the office in the early afternoon, I found Fogerty cursing and yelling at everyone in sight.

"Do you know what that bastard did?" He pointed at me with a rolled-up bunch of newspapers.

"Who?"

"Your goddamn author. His publisher issued a statement today that Horace Jacob Little denies having given an interview. They want to make it look like we made the fucking thing up."

Had we been playing chess, Horace Jacob Little would have placed the *Ledger* in check. It was our word against the word of a shadow. I felt bad for Fogerty, who was taking this personally. The *Ledger* had hired him when he most needed money and self-respect. Despite all the alcohol, he had managed to turn out a good paper for seven years. The statement from Lucent Press could embarrass the newspaper, and him.

"This is why we kept the pictures," he said. "Our asses are covered."

It took me a second to grasp what he was suggesting.

"No," I said. "We can't run them."

"Why not? We had a deal with him, right? Well, he screwed us. Now we screw him."

"I didn't tell you this before, because it didn't seem relevant. Horace Jacob Little threatened me. He said if we ran the pictures he would hold me responsible. He pointed a gun at me. An old antique gun."

Fogerty looked as if he didn't quite believe me. "How about a drink?" he said. "Let's go down to Dignan's and have a drink and figure this thing out."

———

THE NEXT ISSUE of the *Ledger* was being laid out that very day. Fogerty ordered that the existing front-page story be moved inside. In its place, we would have a picture of Horace Jacob Little walking down the street. The picture was taken from behind, as I had followed him, so it showed only a tall figure with wild gray hair and a white shirt. His face and beard were hidden. A caption identified the man as Horace Jacob Little and suggested that the next edition of the *Ledger* would have a photo of his face.

I still had Horace Jacob Little's e-mail address. I sent him a message via Quasar.com: "Check out this week's *Manhattan Ledger*. If you don't acknowledge the validity of our interview, next week we run the face."

His reply was in my inbox when I checked in the morning.

"YOU WIN. CALL OFF THE DOGS. YOU CAN'T BLAME A GUY FOR TRYING."

A new statement came from Lucent Press later that day, correcting the earlier press release and confirming that the interview had indeed been genuine.

"Horace Jacob Little Recognizes Interview," *The New York Times* announced the following morning. "Local Paper Continues to Bedevil Reclusive Author."

chapter fifteen

FROM THE *CONFESSIONS* OF ANDREW WALLACE

Horace Jacob Little would not let me graduate. There were meetings with deans, sessions with doctors, and even a written accusation from the alleged student I had confronted when I noticed her following me. She was posing as an undergrad, and her claim received the undivided attention of the administration. ("The individual grabbed me by the arm and would not let go," etc., etc.) It was all orchestrated from the highest levels of the conspiracy. The doctors tried to convince me I was wrong about Horace Jacob Little, as was their job. They gave me drugs of various colors and sizes, all laced with poison.

I made great progress on my thesis. I had turned it into an accusatory brief detailing the evidence presented in "Strange Meeting" that Horace Jacob Little was guilty of murder. I demanded another thesis advisor after I became aware of Mullin's betrayal. This request was denied, so I continued working without faculty supervision. When I was not at work on the thesis, I wrote countless letters to Lara, pleading with her to reject the false propaganda she had received from Mullin.

In May, I received a letter through campus mail indicating I was to report to the Office of the Dean of Student Affairs. The word "dismissal" figured prominently in the letter. I was not surprised by this move. If anything, I was shocked it had taken Horace Jacob Little so long to arrange my expulsion. Even so, I was devastated to receive the news. I wandered the campus under the half-moon, clutching the letter that was to slam the door shut on the happiness I had known at Princeton. I passed the pelican statue in McCosh courtyard, where I had sat studying for precepts when the weather permitted. I passed the old trees surrounding Prospect Garden, where Lara and I had perched on the gnarled limbs, leaning against each other. I went back to my room at the Grad College and wrote a letter to Lara. For once, I had no desire to interject remarks about Horace Jacob Little. I told her about the meeting at which they were going to send me away. I said that I wished I could have changed the course of events, that I didn't understand what had happened, that I was scared. I asked her to help me, or at least to remember me as I was when we were all that mattered to each other.

THE FIRST KANGAROO court is said to have been held in late-nineteenth-century Australia, where a backwoods madman staged for his own amusement the trial and execution of one of the marsupials. At my own kangaroo court, Mullin was present, as was Dean Peebles, the shrinks and even Professor Wernicke, whom I had not yet linked to the conspiracy. It was made clear that Princeton no longer wanted me on the premises, or more precisely that someone who remained unnamed in that proceeding no longer wanted me on the premises.

I will never forget the moment that Lara opened the door, the dean's secretary in hot pursuit.

—You can't go in there! Dean Peebles is in a meeting.

Lara stood at the doorway, the secretary's head bobbing furiously behind her.

—This is a mistake, Lara said. Andy is a brilliant student who had this place eating out of the palm of his hand. Now he needs help. It isn't right to just throw him out.

I was floored. Lara looked at me, and her gaze contained the entire story of our life together. She had rejected the dictates of my enemies and was ready to stand beside me. My faith in her, in our love and even in myself was instantly restored. If I have ever known a happier moment, I can't recall it.

—And you are? Dean Peebles asked, peering over his reading glasses.

—Lara Knowles, class of ninety-eight. I'm a friend.

I STILL DID not graduate, but that didn't matter. Lara was speaking to me. She insisted on accompanying me to the doctor's office. She forced me to take my medication. I told her it was poisoned, and she could think of no way to prove me wrong but to take a dose herself, which she did.

I knew Lara would be starting law school at NYU in the fall, and therefore I planned to be in New York as well. I decided to spend the summer in the city, finishing my thesis and preparing for Lara's arrival. This would mean enduring weeks without seeing her, but I needed the time to write. The future beckoned with the promise of love among the falling leaves in Central Park, and of walking hand in hand down a Fifth Avenue decked with lights for Christmas. All I had to do was wait out the summer.

Having very little money, I rented an apartment in a former warehouse near the Hudson River, way up in Washington Heights.

The apartment was deplorable, with shabby furniture apparently res-
cued from bankrupt motels, a resident band of fearless roaches,
uncertain hot water, and dusty air that hadn't improved since the
building's previous incarnation as a place for unwanted goods. What
sold me on it, in addition to the cheap rent, was the view of the sunset
from my bedroom window. The sun fell into the Palisades across the
river like a lover racing to an embrace, throwing off trails of pink and
gauzy orange. Whenever I watched the sunset, I remembered that
according to Tacitus, mariners could hear the sun steaming as it fell
into the cool waters at the edge of the world.

WORK ON THE thesis progressed apace. I argued persuasively that
Strange Meeting was the work of a murderer. I analyzed the books
that preceded that collection, theme by theme, word by word, and
contrasted them with the material in *Strange Meeting* and subsequent books, showing conclusively that they were the work of different writers. I included full-color charts and graphs. Horace Jacob
Little's entire oeuvre was an accusation and a confession.

The thesis was, even if it lacked the Princeton imprimatur, a
masterpiece. Proudly, I took a copy to the midtown offices of Horace
Jacob Little's publisher, Lucent Press. I demanded to see the president of the company, but I was told he was unavailable. I left the thesis in the care of the receptionist, who promised to deliver it for me.

I did not expect Lucent to publish it. The house probably already
knew everything it contained, but I wanted to give them a chance to
reject Horace Jacob Little, in case he had managed to deceive them
about some or all of his activities.

I also brought the thesis to Lucent's rival house, Peregrine. Here
too I entrusted a receptionist with the manuscript. I had every expec-
tation that Peregrine would publish it, since to do so would destroy

the rival's star author. It might result in close government scrutiny of Lucent, or even in prosecution, if only the thesis would reach an editor sympathetic to my claims. I sent letters almost every day, addressed to vice-presidents and senior editors, advocating for my manuscript. I sent forgeries from literary agents and politicians calling my work important and impossible to ignore.

I WAS SOON out of money.

I checked with all the small independent bookstores I could find. None of them needed help. The Strand was also fully staffed. I struck gold at the big Upper West Side Barnes & Noble. I joined a staff that seemed to consist entirely of liberal arts majors from the Ivies, the Seven Sisters and the Potted Ivies. I left that day with a plastic name tag that said, "My name is Andrew. How may I help you?"

I liked the summer nights in New York. Walking east along the crosstown blocks, passing tenements barred for fear of criminals, and brownstones stately in their grime, then down Broadway, rushing with traffic, hurried by the scream of angry horns. The temperature and car exhaust transformed the lights into shiny heat curtains, waving like mirages. People strutted and walked, sweaty and half naked. I was gloriously anonymous. I could have been anyone to these people. As I walked down Broadway among businessmen and lovers and middle-aged janitors, I was no one specific. There seemed no chance that Horace Jacob Little and his cohort could find me in that great confluence of anonymity.

But in the city it was impossible to identify Horace Jacob Little's agents. A crowd on Broadway could contain any number of people following me. Every taxi passenger could be reporting on my whereabouts via cell phone. There were videocameras on every block, taking pictures of storefronts and intersections. I knew to whom they were transmitting. Sometimes the crowd would turn ominous, garishly lit by the stream of headlights and the neon signs of all-night delis. Everything was disconnected, the words and laughter of the people harsh and mocking. I would rush home and pick up one of the books purchased with my generous employee discount, then throw it down in frustration and pace my excuse for an apartment, impatient for my waiting time to end.

Meanwhile, new and haunting sights assaulted me. Drug deals disguised as handshakes, homeless people regarding me with moonish, bloodshot eyes that begged for something I couldn't give, prostitutes working the deserted warehouses neighboring the West Side Highway. Sometimes rats would converge on a garbage can, then crawl and rustle through it with abandon. When approached, they would leap away and head for dark corners, only to return within minutes.

Near the West Side Highway, an electronic billboard tallied how much money Americans were saving by selecting a certain long-distance plan. The digital counter ran at an unreadable speed in the hundreds region, the noiseless signal of dollars accumulating in the wallets and pocketbooks of the republic's citizens. The bank accounts for the country must have been under surveillance. Motorists raced beneath the sign through the stagnant summer nights, ignorant of its true significance.

It took some time to become used to the roaches in my apartment. I could hear them skittering around at night. When I switched on the light I would see them, dozens of prehistoric insects, racing for cover. They were on the walls, on the ceiling. They came out of the drain as I showered. They were almost indestructible, absorbing three or four underfoot stomps before their hard shells would break with a crackle.

None of this bothered me. I was physically among that dying world, but mentally secluded in the green and battlemented memories of Princeton with Lara. I could endure that wasteland of car alarms and sad cries in unknown languages because in a few weeks Lara would arrive to dispel the darkness. Without my thoughts of her, though, it would have been easy to grow desperate and frightened.

AND WONDERFUL TO report, she arrived at my door two full months before she was scheduled to move in to a dorm downtown.

—Surprise, she said, and put her hand to my cheek.

I welcomed her to my dark apartment. She said she could stay only briefly.

—My one rule is that we don't talk about Horace Jacob Little, she said.

I was happy to comply. The actions of my enemies were irrelevant when I was with her. We went shopping for food at the local bodega and made a forgettable dinner of packaged paella. After the meal, we reclined on my broken-down sofa, her head on my chest and her hand in mine. I told her about my job, and she said she was happy I was working. She was living at home with her mother for the summer, tanning herself by the family pool.

—I shouldn't be here, she said.

—Why not?

—Never mind. I just had to make sure you were okay.

—I'm okay now that you're here.

She squeezed my hand tighter. A few minutes later, she was gone.

My world was predicated on the idea that Lara would become part of it in the fall, and to have her there for that single day made the rest of the wait even more unendurable. It was like a field trip from prison.

AT NIGHT, ALONE, I found it impossible to sleep. I was scared that I wouldn't wake up. I was scared that I would sleepwalk and slit my wrists in the dirty bathtub. I thought of roaches scurrying across my senseless body, poking into my ears, my mouth, my nose. As I sat awake, other fears tormented me. I feared that things would not fall when I dropped them. I feared that when I picked up books or shoes I would find them too heavy to move. I feared that I would fall through the old floorboards and find a dead body covered in maggots. I feared that I would begin laughing and find myself unable to stop. I feared that I would begin thinking and find myself unable to stop. I feared that I would find the objects in my apartment unrecognizable. Most of all, I feared that I would look in the mirror and find someone other than myself.

WEEKS WENT BY without word from Peregrine. I had sent dozens of letters, as well as additional copies of the manuscript in case it had been misplaced. I called from a pay phone during my breaks at work, and always the people I spoke with professed ignorance.

I came to suspect that Lucent and Peregrine were not, in fact, rivals, but rather twin arms of the same conspiracy. This suspicion was confirmed when shipments from the two companies began arriving at Barnes & Noble simultaneously every few days.

It came down to a simple fact: Horace Jacob Little had total control of the publishers and would not let my thesis get anywhere near a printing press.

This angered me, but I was powerless to change anything. I spent long nights pondering the situation. I toyed with the idea of printing copies of the thesis myself on a Xerox machine and handing them out on the subway. I called a few TV news organizations, but they too seemed to be under his control. I dreamed of finding Horace Jacob Little and confronting him directly, but the world was organized in an attempt to hide him.

Finally I sought an answer in the weapon of the powerless, civil disobedience. It was my best hope to draw attention to the truth.

I bought a large knife intended for the carving of meat. On a day off from work, I took the knife to the office of Lucent Press. I presented myself to the receptionist, and demanding once again to see the president of the company, I put the knife to my throat and threatened to kill myself.

I should assure my reader that I was not prepared to do any such thing. It was a bluff, and it worked.

—Don't! the receptionist shrieked. Hold on! I'll get Mr. Sorenson.

Mr. Sorenson appeared, and I was able to make a full statement of my grievances. It was comprehensive but succinct, and I left before the police could be summoned.

CHAPTER SIXTEEN

Sitting in the Cafarellas' place watching TV, I was surprised by a late-night knock on the door. I found Andrew Wallace in the hallway. I did not immediately recognize him. His hair was neatly cut and combed. He was well dressed, in stylish black pants and a freshly pressed white shirt. The lenses of his glasses were spotless, and the clear pupils were watching me hopefully.

My first thought was of Lara. If Andrew was in town and he had come to see me, a relatively minor player in his private drama, then surely he had visited Lara. Maybe he had stalked her again, or threatened her. It might not be such a good thing to have Andrew Wallace on my doorstep. I couldn't see his hands, which were clasped behind him. Perhaps he saw the concern on my face, because he brought them into view and said, "I'm better. Modern medicine has triumphed once again."

It had been a while since I'd visited him, and he certainly looked recovered. Andrew had always reminded me of a slightly crazed stockbroker, and now he looked like a sane one. Even if he wasn't entirely better, I didn't have the heart to shut the door in his face.

"I hope I'm not bothering you," he said as he took a seat on the Cafarellas' couch. "I found your address in the alumni directory."

Jimmy, the ordinarily aloof cat who was under my care, emerged from the kitchen, sauntered over to Andrew and allowed himself to be stroked.

"Nice cat. Yours?"

"He belongs to the people I'm subletting from."

"The Cafarellas?"

It occurred to me in a terrible instant that, appearances be damned, Andrew Wallace might still be crazy. If he knew the name of the lease-holders he might have been conducting research on me, following me around.

"How did you know their name?"

"It was on the mailbox downstairs." He smiled as if to reassure me he meant no harm.

"So writing an autobiography brought you back to reality."

"Actually, I think it's this new drug they started giving me. Although the writing may have helped. It certainly kept my mind busy."

Jimmy jumped up on the couch and began purring and snuggling against Andrew's leg.

"You're probably wondering why I'm here."

I shrugged, not wanting to seem rude.

"I'm trying to go around and visit some of the people who saw me when I was sick. Imagine you met someone when you were really drunk and made a fool of yourself. Imagine you were so out of it you didn't even remember what you said or did, but only had a vague impression the next morning that you had disgraced yourself. That's how I feel. I wanted to try to negate that first impression."

"There's no need. I completely understand."

"No, this is important to me. You were nice enough to come visit me at the hospital, and I said crazy things to you about Horace Jacob Little. I want to put all that stuff in the past."

I was in an awkward position. By tracking Horace Jacob Little, I had connected myself to the very person at the center of Andrew's obsessions. He had accused me of working for Horace Jacob Little, and lo and behold, a few weeks later the interview appeared.

"You mentioned at the hospital that I should be investigating Horace Jacob Little. The funny thing is, I did what you suggested."

"I heard about the interview on the news. I haven't read it yet. Could I see it?"

I didn't want to show it to him, but it was hardly classified information. I rummaged through some back issues of the *Ledger* and gave him the paper. He read the article in silence.

"I'm not working for Horace Jacob Little," I said. "You do believe me?"

"Oh, I'm beyond all that. I just wonder what he was like, that's all."

"I promised him I wouldn't talk about the interview. That was part of the deal. I've been getting calls asking about him ever since."

He scratched Jimmy behind the ears, and this delighted the cat.

"Can I have a glass of water? The medicine I'm on makes me ridiculously thirsty."

I rose and went into the kitchen. Jimmy followed me and sat by his supper dish looking hopeful, so I fed him while I was there.

"You know," I said when I returned with the water, "I've read your autobiography. I feel like I know so much about you."

"That wasn't really me. I was totally confused when I wrote it. This is the real me."

The disclaimer struck me as unfortunate. Of course I was glad if Andrew had been cured of his illness, but I kind of enjoyed the old Andrew, the one in the *Confessions*.

"It's late," he said. "I don't want to keep you."

"Where are you staying now?"

He pressed his lips together and looked at the floor. "I'm at a cheap hotel in the Bronx. Dr. Saunders gave me a little money when they discharged me, but I'm in a bad situation."

"What do you mean?"

"I'm trying to get a job before my money runs out."

I felt a strong affinity for Andrew. We both had gone to Princeton. We both had at various times been infatuated with Lara Knowles. We both were interested in Horace Jacob Little. We even looked somewhat alike. What small tangle of overactive or underactive neurons had pushed him over the edge into madness, while I hung back? But for blind chance, it could have been me standing there trying to find a way back to reality.

"You don't owe me anything," he said. "But I could really use a favor. If you've read my autobiography, you know all about Lara. You know how much she means to me. The problem is, I can't just march up to her and announce that I'm better. She would be scared. She wouldn't believe me. It would really make things easier if you could get in touch with her and tell her I'm in New York. Tell her I'm better. That way when I see her she'll know."

He was right. I didn't owe him anything. But I did owe Lara something. I had not spoken with her for about a month—not since that night we kissed and fought and I realized how much she missed Andrew. Before that night, I would have politely rejected Andrew's request for help. I would have thought, *Hey, with Andrew out of the picture I have a better shot with Lara.* But I'd already had my shot, and missed. I still cared enough about Lara that I wanted her to be happy.

I told him, "Of course. I'll tell her."

After Andrew left I sat down to read some notes for a story I was planning to work on the next day. My notebook wasn't in my bag, where I thought I had put it. I looked everywhere in the apartment, even in the bureau drawer I habitually avoided because it contained Mr. Cafarella's "home security system"—a revolver and a box of bullets. I eventually located the notebook, buried under the cushions of the couch. I tried to work but I couldn't concentrate, so I called Lara.

"What makes you think I want to get back together with Andy?" she said.

"Even if he was the same as when you first met him?"

"I've grown up since then. Anyway, I can't forget everything that went in between. I understand what you're trying to do. I appreciate it, but I don't need a matchmaker."

I was frustrated by her reaction. There I was, trying to do the right thing and put aside my own feelings and interests, and she sounded annoyed by my intervention.

"If you see him, you can do whatever you want," I said. "I'm just saying you don't need to run away."

"YOU HAVE TO understand," Lara told me when I met her for lunch at the Boathouse Café in Central Park three weeks later, "I was trying so hard to get on with my life. I told myself Andy belonged in my past and I should leave it at that. A few days after your call I got a letter from him. It was very simple. It said he was living in the Bronx and feeling better with this new drug. He said he would understand if I didn't want to see him. He wanted to see me, though, whenever I thought it would be okay. That was it. Only a few sentences. There was nothing crazy in it. He didn't use crazy language or strange words. He signed it 'Yours, Andy,' rather than 'Love.' He didn't go on for pages and pages about the depth of his love for me. If he had done that I would never have gone to see him."

We were sitting near the lake on a summery September afternoon. An umbrella over the table sheltered us from the sun, and Lara's sunglasses were perched in her blond hair, serving as a headband. The top of her head was bathed in sunlight that escaped the umbrella. Her sunglasses and hair shone brilliantly.

"So you're glad I called?"

"I'm sorry I was rude. I didn't know how to handle it. But if you hadn't called to say he was better, I wouldn't have believed his note."

Rowboats sent noises across the lake, the clunk of oarlocks, the splash of oars, the voices of rowers and passengers.

"You went up to his place?"

"We spent the night sitting on his couch, talking, like we used to do at school. He lit a bunch of candles and we sat in the candlelight. We talked about everything. We ended up talking about life. I guess that sounds odd, but after being there for a few hours I felt I could reflect on everything that had happened to me and to him and to us. It was like I had left my old life behind. We didn't do anything. We didn't immediately get back together. We just talked until the sun came up."

Lara had asked me to meet her at the café. Andrew was to show up at some point, and the two of them were to walk around the park. I was glad she had invited me. It was partly a lunch to say thank you for my help with Andrew. It was also, I understood, a lunch to put to rest whatever hard feelings and awkwardness might linger between us. As Lara narrated the events of her past few weeks, I felt nothing but happiness for her. I was not jealous. I did not want her to lean across the table and whisper, *But it's really you I want, Jake.* I was simply thrilled to see her so enthused and animated.

When Andrew arrived she saw him first. She was looking over my shoulder and suddenly her eyes were awake, doing their best to capture every detail of the world around her. I turned to see Andrew approaching our table. He wore a black T-shirt and black jeans. He placed a hand on my back and shook my hand, then kissed Lara and took a seat.

"My two favorite people in New York," he said. He looked out at the lake and took a deep breath, the way a mountain climber might survey the world from a summit.

"Life is good," he said. "Hey, I caught your article about police brutality last week. It's a subject near to my heart, as you can imagine. I liked the way you alternated between interviews with the police captain and with that family—the Joneses?"

"Thanks," I said. I was proud of the article. It had run on the the first page of the *Ledger* and had gotten lots of compliments. Captain Higgins was the guy I had met with to talk about complaints of excessive force, and the Joneses' son, Patrick, had recently died in police custody. The article consisted of their words, juxtaposed. It made me think I might have a future in journalism after all.

"Did you bring the food?" Lara asked Andrew.

"Right here," he said, lifting his backpack from under the table. "A three-course meal. And a blanket and wine and candles and a book of Shakespeare's sonnets."

Andrew could do nothing with moderation—not love Lara or write a personal history or, as in this case, plan a picnic. Everything had to be grand, larger than life. There was a tinge of mania at the root of his personality, deeper than his madness, deeper than the drugs could touch.

"I'd better get back to the office," I said. They protested, but I insisted. I had some writing to do. I also wanted to leave the two of them alone. Lara put the Knowles money to good use by picking up the check. I left them at the lake as they strolled northward, hand in hand, close together and engrossed in conversation.

THAT NIGHT THERE was a burglary at the *Ledger*. I entered the office the following morning to find the staff standing in groups, murmuring amid the disorder. Desks had been overturned. Drawers had been emptied onto the floor and their contents violently dispersed. The computers were missing.

"Do you have your notes?" Fogerty sputtered when he saw me. "We've lost your story for this week. It was on a disk that's somewhere in that pile of shit over there and on the hard drive of the computer that used to be right here."

"I can rewrite it," I said. "No problem."

"Everything's gone." He put his hands on his hips and scanned the room. "All our ads, all our files, all the clippings I've been keeping for thirty years. What the hell could someone want with that stuff? The computers I can understand, but the rest?"

"What about the Horace Jacob Little pictures?" I asked.

"Gone."

It had been well over a month since we had threatened Horace Jacob Little with publication of a frontal photo. It made a lot of sense for him to take that picture out of our hands.

I laughed at myself. Andrew had been granted a reprieve from his delusions, and I was picking up where he left off, blaming every event on the secret machinations of Horace Jacob Little. Still, I had to wonder: What kind of burglar would disappear into the night with a half-dozen filing cabinets?

chapter seventeen

The ringing of the phone catapulted me from sleep. Stranded between dreaming and awareness, I found the noise intolerably loud, and my first thought was to stop it as quickly as possible. I leaped out of bed and stumbled across the bedroom, stubbing my toe on the bedpost in my haste.

"Jake?" a voice said. "It's Andy. Andy Wallace."

"What time is it?"

"I think it's about two. I didn't wake you, did I?"

"What's wrong?" I had not spoken to either Andrew or Lara in several weeks. My first thought was that something had happened to her.

"Nothing's wrong. In fact, everything is right. I've got a great story for you, your biggest one yet."

"What?"

"I'm going to give this to you to write up in the *Ledger*. You don't even have to share the byline with me. Just quote me here and there. I'll have a few good sound bites for you. Like, 'I always knew Horace Jacob Little was a malign force in this society.' "

"What are you talking about?" My heart sank. "Have you been taking your medicine?"

"That's enough for now. I'll reveal the rest in good time. I'm sure they bugged your phone after you published the interview with him. I'll catch you later."

He hung up. I stood in the darkness of the bedroom, the receiver in my hand. I knew I would not be able to fall asleep again. I was fully awake, my mind reeling with Andrew's rapid-fire words.

"The poor bastard," I said aloud. Jimmy the cat looked at me, stretched and fell back asleep, blissfully ignorant of human words, meanings and misinterpretations.

IN THE MORNING I called Lara to tell her what had happened.

"I don't even want to talk to you," she said.

"Why not?"

"Because you ruined everything. Of course Andy had a relapse. You gave him the fucking address. Just leave me alone. Have a nice life."

"Wait. Don't hang up. What address?"

"Andy had a piece of paper with Horace Jacob Little's address written in your handwriting. How could you?"

"That's impossible."

"I remember what your handwriting looks like. It had other stuff scribbled on the back."

"Oh my God," I said, but she had already hung up.

I went to the shelf that contained all the notebooks I had used since I started at the *Ledger*. I flipped through them until I found the one from July. Horace Jacob Little's address, I remembered, was on the first page of my transcription of the interview. The top part of that page, the little strip of paper around the holes, was still there, trapped by the silver coils. But the rest was gone. It had been torn out.

I remembered that during Andrew's unexpected visit that night, I had left the room for about two minutes, getting him a glass of water and feeding Jimmy. While I was in the kitchen, Andrew must have gone through my notebook and ripped out the address.

I sat on the couch, staring in amazement at the notebook that had potentially changed the course of two lives. I knew from the *Confessions* how unhappy Andrew was when beset by his invisible enemies. Now, through my own stupidity, I had sent him down that road again. Lara was furious with me, and she was right.

I imagined Andrew standing outside Horace Jacob Little's apartment building. I tried to place myself in his state of mind. He would probably lie low for a few days, stalking Horace Jacob Little. Then he would confront him. He would accuse him of murdering the first Horace Jacob Little. He would use "Strange Meeting" as evidence. Andrew might even try to act out the story. If Horace Jacob Little was Seamus Small, then Andrew might see himself as Evan Doherty.

I bolted from the apartment and got on the subway to Manhattan, heading to Lara's. I was probably the last person she wanted to see at that moment, but I knew she wouldn't speak to me on the phone, and I had to get Andrew's address.

"WHAT DO YOU want?" Lara peeked out from the barely open door, above a taut chain lock. She wasn't scared I was a burglar, since the security guard had called up to announce me. She just didn't want to let me in.

"I want to explain what happened," I said.

She adopted an incredulous look. "Go ahead," she said, still hiding behind the door.

"I came all the way over here. Can't I come in?"

She glared at me for a second before unhooking the chain and opening the door.

"We started classes this week. I'm studying. I don't have much time to spare."

Her dorm room was in a state of hyperorganization. It looked like something a real estate agent might dream up to show clients. Even her books and papers, which were spread out on the couch, were grouped into neat piles and binders. Either event—the start of the school year or the mental collapse of a loved one—would have thrown me and my surroundings into chaos. Lara's reaction was to deny herself the privilege of disorder. She was dressed in full-length blue silk pajamas and was drinking from a large mug of tea.

"I'm listening," she said.

I told her about Andrew's visit. I showed her what was left of the notebook page he had torn. She sighed and sat down.

"The side effects of the medicine were getting worse and worse," she said. "He was shaking and moving uncontrollably. He said it was like being electrocuted."

"He stopped taking his medication?"

"No. He said he would take it no matter what the side effects if it meant staying in control of his life. It just stopped working. He went out to the bookstore and bought a whole collection of Horace Jacob Little books, which I threw away without telling him. Then he said Horace Jacob Little had people break into his apartment to steal the books. It got even worse from there."

She took a drink of tea.

"How could you have been so careless?" she said, now showing a flash of emotion. "After all, you knew about Andy."

"I thought he was better. Maybe this is only a passing thing. Maybe if he gets a higher dose of the medicine or something."

Lara stared at the floor and nodded. "I've done this before," she said. "I've waited for him to get better. I've gone after him, brought him to doctors, forced him to take drugs. I don't know if I can do it again."

She looked as if she hadn't slept in a while. She was speaking not with anger or sadness, but in exhaustion. I wanted to sit next to her and let her fall asleep against my body.

"I need his address."

"You're going to visit him?" she asked, before opening a black book to copy out the information.

"I want to make everything right again. I'm worried that—" I stopped short. There was no need to burden Lara with the remote possibility of violence.

"Worried that what?"

I got up to leave, but she grabbed my arm and wouldn't let me go until I told her. "What if he tries to act out the story?" I said.

"What do you mean?"

"Evan Doherty kills the twin in the end."

Her grip tightened around my arm. She bit her lower lip and closed her eyes.

"No," she said, doing her best not to cry. She pushed me into the hallway and slammed the door.

AT THE OFFICE that morning, I was not surprised when a fellow reporter told me, "Mr. Horace on line three."

I collected my thoughts before I picked up the phone. Although I had been thinking of nothing else since the night before, I still didn't know what to tell him.

"You lying piece of shit," he said when I picked up.

I decided to play dumb. "Who is this?"

"Someone's been following me around for the past three days. I know you think this is a big game set up for your own amusement, but let me tell you something. This is not a game. This is my life."

"I'm afraid this has nothing to do with me."

"No one has ever known who I was or where I lived. Then you find me, run an interview, and now I have some nutcase following me around. He broke into my apartment and stole a bunch of stuff, including some pages of the novel I'm working on. You're telling me this is a coincidence?"

I had to warn him. I would never have forgiven myself if anything happened to Horace Jacob Little before I had the chance to find Andrew.

"Okay," I said. "I'll level with you. Your address may have fallen into the hands of a disturbed fan. I'm going to take care of everything. Just stay out of harm's way for a while."

Horace Jacob Little did not explode with anger, as I had expected. He said plaintively, "He threatened to kill me. Why?"

"He has delusions about you. He thinks you've been tracking him for years. He thinks 'Strange Meeting' is based on a true story."

"Based on a true story?"

"Never mind. Let me fix this."

I TOOK THE rest of the day off from work, telling Fogerty I was going out to interview someone at the Board of Ed. Instead, I rode the subway up to Andrew's neighborhood, which first appeared to consist of nothing but factories in various states of neglect. Some were in full operation, with trucks backing up to loading docks amid the rumbling machines. Others were boarded up and covered with graffiti. I passed vacant lots where tall weeds surrounded junked refrigerators, then a basketball court with no hoops, and a row of busy auto-body shops.

I came to an enclave of grimy five-story apartment buildings, some of which were abandoned. Andrew's building was so filthy I couldn't determine the bricks' original color. Lara told me he had moved here from his hotel soon after they had gotten back together.

The label next to his buzzer was blank. I pressed the button and waited. Nothing happened. I pressed it a few more times and began to wonder whether Lara had given me the right address and apartment number.

Finally Andrew appeared behind the locked foyer door. He opened it and said, "Are you alone?"

"Your buzzer doesn't work?"

"No, it's fine. I don't want to let people up when I can't see them first. Are you sure no one followed you?"

"Positive. We need to talk."

"Not here!" He held up his hand to silence me. He pointed to the dirty light fixture and then to his ear.

We went outside and he whispered, "The whole place is bugged."

"I know you took the address," I said as we walked down the deserted street.

"I'm sorry. I had to see him for myself. You won't be upset when you hear the story I've found for you. 'Famous Author's Checkered Past.' By Jake Burnett." He still spoke in a low voice, leaning toward my ear.

"Horace Jacob Little is an unpredictable man. If you keep bothering him, he'll get very angry. He may try to hurt you. Or me."

"Now you're catching on!"

"That's not what I meant—"

Andrew had dyed his hair jet black. He had a three- or four-day beard, and he wore jogging pants and a tie-dyed shirt.

"I know this sounds crazy," he said. "It's different this time. I swear."

"Do you understand that all of this is upsetting Lara?"

"She'll come back to me once I prove everything. In fact, I'll be her hero for valiantly exposing the truth. I need your help to get this message out to the *Ledger*'s readership."

"But you're not seeing the truth. You may need a higher dose of your medication. I'm going to bring you back to Overlook."

I expected an argument, but Andrew smiled and nodded rapidly. "That's exactly where I wanted to take you! While we're there I want you to interview a patient named Earl Jenkins. Then if you still think I'm crazy, maybe I really am."

cHapTer eIGHTeen

At the end of that summer, Lara arrived in New York to begin law school. She had not spoken to me or sent a letter in more than a month. I worried that my enemies had again confused her with false claims about me.

Rather than approach her as soon as she arrived, I decided that the most logical strategy was to stay hidden for a few days. Let her become accustomed to her new life. I would have to do background research.

Lara walked out of her dorm with three other people. One was a broad-chested guy who walked with a swagger and wore a leather jacket. The other girl had long black hair and spoke with animation, although from a distance I could not hear what she said. The final member of the group was a man caught between being clean-shaven and bearded, and the half-shadow on his face made him look sullen.

By this time I too had grown a beard. It was easier than shaving all the time. I hated the way the razor felt against my skin, and I was unable to stop thinking that even a tiny slip in the wrong direction would part the skin and bring blood gushing unstoppably.

They walked north toward Fourteenth Street, chattering and laughing and dividing into pairs as they made their way around competing pedestrians. From my distance behind them I was able to catch only isolated words. The guy in the leather jacket was named Glen. He was concentrating the bulk of his attention on Lara.

They stopped at a pool hall south of Fourteenth Street. I ascended the creaky stairs in their wake, noticing the increasing ratio of smoke to oxygen as we neared the top, where the stairway opened into a room ghostly with cigarette smoke and housing maybe fifty pool tables. Lara and her friends took a table at the back. I selected another across the room and pretended to play a game against myself; I turned off the light above the table and covered myself in darkness. As far as I knew, Lara had no idea how to play pool. She certainly had never mentioned it to me and had shown no interest in it at Princeton. To my surprise, she bent over the table with a practiced air, threaded the cue through the circle of her spectacular fingers and sank two balls in a row.

Glen was her partner. I could see even from across the room where his real interest in the evening lay. It was after their second game that Lara and her companions procured a round of beers. I thought for sure Lara would pass. Instead she eagerly grasped one of the bottles and lifted it to her lips, then jerked the bottom confidently for a sip. She laughed and played and stood very close to Glen. As the night wore on, I noticed that buttons were becoming undone on her blouse, although I did not see her fiddling with them. Underneath she wore a revealing piece of loose fabric supported by small straps over each shoulder and invitingly open on the bottom.

After the pool hall they headed to a bar. Again, I followed them and placed myself in a darkened corner, observing from afar.

That's when the real fun began. The bar was having a special on tequila shots, and I watched as Lara sprinkled salt on her wrist and licked it sensually, looking all the while at Glen. She took the shot glass delicately between thumb and index finger, threw it to her lips with a backward toss of the head and followed with a suck on a quartered lime. Glen did likewise, looking at Lara in the same suggestive way. Quickly, even before I had finished the Coke I had ordered, Lara had downed three shots. Music came from an invisible source, insistent and upbeat. Lara swayed gently and Glen put his hands on her hips, as I used to do.

Lara and Glen decided, with a series of intimate whispers made necessary by the loud music, that they would go home. They left the other two, who had fallen into a strained silence punctuated by sudden outbursts from the black-haired girl, and made their way to the door. Glen's hand rested gently on the small of Lara's back as they walked slowly, enjoying the night, speaking leisurely. They disappeared at the door to her dormitory, to continue their evening rituals upstairs in privacy.

These revelations had been entirely unexpected.

I walked back uptown, a phrase beating in my head: *Something terrible has happened. Something terrible has happened.* Lara was with someone new. Even worse, she was acting like a stranger. There was no more wide-eyed acceptance of the world's offerings. She was indistinguishable from the dozens of other twenty-something women at the bar. I had no idea what to do. Without Lara, there was no one on earth who really cared about me. No one. I needed her back, but the gravity that had drawn us together no longer seemed in effect.

WORK AT BARNES & NOBLE was not glamorous or noteworthy, but it did pay the bills and allow me to live in some proximity to my lost Lara. I spent most of the time shelving books. Only when we were shorthanded would I work checkout. The management wanted to limit my contact with the customers, which was fine with me. I was in no mood to deal with people.

Frequently authors would come to the store to do readings and question-and-answer sessions. Troops of fans would dutifully gather and fill the folding chairs we set up beforehand. The questions were about the technical details of writing:

—How do you write?

—Where do you write?

—When do you write?

—Where do you get your ideas?

Sometimes, just for fun, I would stand in the back and ask questions about the influence of the Oulipo movement or Kristeva that would puzzle everyone, authors included. My co-workers started calling me "The Professor," not without some contempt.

As I worked I kept a close eye on who was buying the Horace Jacob Little books. Those books were the perfect tool for underground communications between the author and his agents. A few misprints in a given book could constitute a code whereby orders would be passed to the subordinates. I bought many, many copies of his books from the store. At home I would compare them all, word by word, looking for letters or sentences that were out of place.

I also stuck notecards in the Horace Jacob Little books on the store's shelves. These explained to unsuspecting consumers the truth about the author. I warned them not to buy the book unless they wanted to risk being swept up in Horace Jacob Little's system of surveillance.

I spoke to a few people browsing through the section, hoping to detect their affiliations. My boss got wind of this and threatened to fire me.

A BLUSTERY DAY brought Professor Mullin into the store. I was not surprised. I had been expecting his appearance. I knew he would eventually emerge and once again seek to turn my life upside down. After these months of relative peace and quiet, my enemies were opening a new offensive. Mullin did not see me at first, so I sneaked around the shelves, following him from section to section.

He selected a book in the history section and took a seat in one of the comfy armchairs. I approached and stood before him.

—Andrew, he said, rising to his feet. He pretended to be taken aback.

—What are you doing here?

—I'm just passing through.

—Did he send you here to keep track of me?

—I don't know what you're talking about. Let's relax.

—Don't tell me to fucking relax, I yelled. You leave me alone and I'll relax.

Everyone was watching us. It was not enough that they had destroyed my life at Princeton. They were going to run me out of New York as well. I imagined Mullin had already been to see Lara, to make sure I could not win her back. They had trapped me. I saw in Mullin's eyes that they would never let me go.

I swiped my arm at a shelf next to him, and brought dozens of books crashing to the floor. Mullin jumped away with a terrified look. I went for another shelf, and another. The books flew through the air.

—Just leave me alone, I was saying. Just leave me alone, you bas-tards! I want my life back.

My boss made me clean up the mess before she fired me.

I CALLED PRINCETON'S Department of Comparative Literature and asked to speak to Professor Mullin. I was not surprised when the secretary said:

—He's at Columbia University now.

I hung up before she could continue. Mullin had been sent to New York to keep closer tabs on me. I had two choices. I could leave New York and hide somewhere. I pictured myself living in a fishing village on the coast of Maine. I thought of going out to California, to the wine country to pick grapes with the migrant workers. What guarantee did I have, though, that Mullin and Horace Jacob Little wouldn't follow me?

My other choice was to fight back. Throwing the books around at Barnes & Noble had felt good. Mullin had looked scared of me. Thus far the war had been conducted with words. The gathering of intelli-gence was at its heart.

It was time to escalate the conflict.

It is difficult to find a sledgehammer in Manhattan hardware stores. I had to go all the way out to Queens to find one. I noticed a security camera pointing at me as I paid for it, so I told the clerk that I intended to take down a wall in my apartment.

I HUNG AROUND the Columbia campus with the sledgehammer par-tially concealed in a duffel bag too small to hide it completely. I didn't want to stay in one place for fear someone would identify me, so I walked quickly and constantly. I also combed my hair over my face to hide my identity.

I saw Mullin walking down the steps of Low Library and I followed him to an apartment building on Riverside Drive. I moved my stakeout to a location in the park across the street.

By the next day I had identified Mullin's car, a dusty Volvo parked on the street near the building. I put the first phase of my plan into effect.

Using a can of spray paint, I festooned the car with accusations. SPY! HEARTWRECKER! MURDERER! HORACE JACOB LITTLE MUST BE STOPPED!

Then I took out the sledgehammer. I pounded the car again and again, until the windshield was a spider web of safety glass, the top of the car wrinkled like a piece of paper, the roof collapsed and toppled, the doors ravaged as though collided with on all sides. Headlights destroyed, trunk demolished. I took out a knife and stabbed the tires. It was pure ecstasy. Pain and anger and confusion and loneliness had been stewing inside me for months, and at last I could release them. I worked toward catharsis, concentrating intently on every blow, every dent. A police car arrived just as the front bumper fell to the ground.

I dropped the sledgehammer and ran, but one of the officers had a jump on me. He tackled me and brought me to the sidewalk hard enough that I blacked out.

WAKING FROM UNCONSCIOUSNESS was an amazing experience. I was first aware of voices around me, even before I was aware of myself. I knew I was lying down. I was not disturbed or confused by my situation or by my lack of knowledge regarding it. My self, my ego, had temporarily shut down. My soul had descended to the region of nonexistence, where the erstwhile multiple souls of my childhood had gone. I was dreaming without dreaming. I opened my eyes to an enclosed room that was shaking back and forth. A plastic tube dangled from the ceiling and snaked toward my arm. A voice behind me was talking about blood pressure. Then it said:

—He's awake. Sir, can you tell me your name?

I was strapped to a stretcher. I struggled with the restraints.

—We're taking you to the hospital. Can you tell me your name?

—I won't tell you anything, I said.

When we got to the hospital, a doctor shined a light in my eyes and barked questions at me. I kept my mouth shut and tried to undo the restraints. They injected a drug into the IV line and for the second time that day I lost myself in unconsciousness.

THEY BROUGHT ME to the hospital because the cop had knocked me out. They said I had a concussion. An exhausted-looking medical student came to talk to me. Pens, books and notes bulged out of every pocket of his white coat. He asked me about Mullin's car.

I explained that the destruction of the car was an act of self-defense and civil disobedience, the first public exposé of a system of deception erected by Horace Jacob Little. I explained how the original author had been murdered and replaced by the man we now call Horace Jacob Little. I told the student that Mullin was following me under orders from the author.

—Okay, I'm going to have a doctor from the psychiatry department come down to talk to you.

—Sure, I said.

As I waited for the shrink, I realized I had already said too much. The cops had arrived only a few minutes after I started attacking the car. They might have had advance knowledge of my intended action. They might not even have been real police officers. They could have been working for Horace Jacob Little. They must have been watching me and waiting for me to make a move. It was all a setup. The ambulance had not been a real ambulance. I was not in a real hospital. This was not a real medical student. I was strapped to a stretcher surrounded by agents of Horace Jacob Little and totally at his mercy.

THEY WOULD NOT let me leave. The fake psychiatrist admitted me against my wishes. They kept me in a small gray room with a grate over the dirty window, and a door that was kept locked. My first night there, I heard someone laughing hysterically in another room. Several minutes passed before I recognized with a shudder that the person was crying, not laughing. There was nothing to do but lie in bed all day and night, thinking.

They were constantly injecting drugs into me and asking me questions. I kept my mouth shut, like a cool, hardened criminal with silence on his side. Every so often I would ask them:

—How do I know this is a real hospital?

They could only scowl and lock the door.

AFTER I HAD lost track of the days, a short, elderly man appeared at the door. He walked with a four-toed cane.

—Who are you? I asked.

—My name is Dr. Saunders.

He spoke quietly and evenly, in a voice that requested trust.

—I want you to know that you're free to go. Professor Mullin has declined to press charges. The doctors here have given you medicine to help you, and they will continue to do so. You can walk right out that door anytime you want. Before you go, I want to tell you about where I'm from. I'm the director of a home for artists and writers.

—Is that where Horace Jacob Little lives?

—No, but it's where you could live. I hear that you went to Princeton, and that you like to write.

—Sometimes.

—What do you write?

—Stories. Philosophical notes. Whatever comes to mind.

—Why don't you come with me for a while? The hospital is upstate. All these difficulties with Horace Jacob Little will be over. Perhaps you'd like to write your autobiography?

The thought appealed to me, intoxicated me. To be free from this thickening web of suspicion and intrigue, to write, to tell my own story. It was the perfect way to strike back. I would write up my experiences so that they could be passed from person to person, or maybe even published. Horace Jacob Little would be powerless to stop my words once they were released to the world. Of course, Dr. Saunders could have been sent by Horace Jacob Little, but it made no difference. If this writers' colony was where Horace Jacob Little wanted me to be, I would end up there whether or not I cooperated.

AN AMBULETTE DROVE me upstate to the Overlook Psychiatric Institute, also known as the Muse Asylum. It was housed in a mansion perched on the slope of a hill in backwoods New York. Below was a small town called Overlook, the main feature of which was a towering smokestack standing sentry above an abandoned chemical factory.

Dr. Saunders met me and took me on a tour. He said many of the rooms on the first floor of the mansion were unchanged from the time the Benderson family lived there. I ran my hands over the silk-covered pillows on the formal couches, peered at myself in the enormous gold-framed mirror above a marble fireplace and stretched out on the window seat overlooking the rolling lawn and babbling backyard fountain. I had never, even at Princeton, been surrounded by such opulence.

—Here? I asked in disbelief. I'm going to be living here?

Dr. Saunders smiled and showed me to my room on the second floor, which was, despite the glorious decor I had seen downstairs, a small white cell with a standard metal bed frame. In one corner sat a table with a stack of paper and two felt-tipped pens arranged in parallel on top.

There was no sense wasting time. I moved the table close to the window so I could look out over the valley. I picked up a pen and began to write.

CHapTer nineTeen

Andrew was standing on a street corner, wearing several layers of clothing and a coat, which made his arms look bulky and tubular. He still needed to shave and his hair was uncombed. Purple sunglasses hid his eyes.

"Get in the car," I said when he hesitated. "It's me."

"Are you sure no one followed you?"

"Positive."

I saw no harm in humoring him. Of course, I hadn't paid the slightest attention to the cars around me. Of the dozens of identical taxis behind me, theoretically any one could have followed me unnoticed.

I had rented the car that morning for the excursion to Overlook. For the first few minutes of the trip, Andrew fidgeted in his seat, played with the temperature controls, flipped the sun visor up and down, and wrestled with his seat belt. He located the car manual after rummaging through the glove compartment and found it to be of consuming interest. Every so often he would read a sentence from it. "The oil dipstick is located behind the carburetor, marked by a red handle." "When sliding on ice, steer into the curve." "Maintaining proper tire pressure will significantly improve gas mileage." When he tired of the book he offered non sequiturs: "That's the fourth license plate we've seen from Washington state." "I wonder if the buffalo ever roamed wild here."

Somewhere near Albany, he said, "Have you ever heard of Josef Mengele?"

"The Nazi?"

"The Angel of Death. He was the doctor in charge of human experimentation at Auschwitz. He was obsessed with twins. He thought they contained the solution to the mystery of genetics. Whenever a pair of twins arrived, he'd take them away to a special barracks where 'his' children lived. And then he would subject them to surgeries and injections and psychological tests. It's said he made fraternal twins copulate."

"Why are you telling me this?"

"I was reading a book about him yesterday. The most diabolical thing is that Mengele could torture people and still pretend to care about them. He would give the children candy and hug them and have them call him Uncle Mengele. Then he would vivisect them."

Andrew fell silent for a few moments, staring at the passing trees, road signs, scarred walls of rock.

"After the war he disappeared. Into thin air. They found a grave in South America in the mid-eighties that's supposedly his, but there's no way to tell for sure. He disappeared, just like Horace Jacob Little."

"If Mengele were alive, he would be an old man. Horace Jacob Little is not Josef Mengele."

"I'm not suggesting that. I'm simply pointing out an interesting correspondence. Twins, evil deeds, strange disappearances."

I turned up the radio and drove on, frustrated by Andrew's wild talk and my inability to convince him of its unsoundness. He was not being totally illogical, but there was a strain of paranoia in his willingness to discover the unexpected connection. I changed lanes and passed several cars with a satisfying burst of acceleration.

"Have you ever heard of split-brain patients?" he continued. "The right and left hemispheres of the brain are severed, and the right and left halves of the body begin to function independently of each other. The right hand will reach for an object only to find that the left hand has already grabbed it."

We had been on the road for several hours, and I wondered whether Andrew needed to take his medicine.

"I don't need that stuff," he said. "Rydazine makes me feel terrible. Nauseous, sweaty, anxious. No thank you, sir."

I was heartened by a sign for Overlook. We were nearing our destination after hours of traveling and what seemed like days, weeks, months of preparation. How had I gotten myself involved in this plot, spiriting away a lunatic to a mental hospital in upstate New York to save us both from the wrath of the reclusive master of the modern novel? Andrew, poor Andrew beside me, my misguided classmate—his resurrection was about to end. He was about to be doomed once again to a sequestered life in that old madhouse of a mansion.

As we approached Overlook, the Benderson smokestack came into view, looming over the barren town like a rocket ship abandoned by its inventors.

"I've decided my favorite Horace Jacob Little story is 'The History of London,' " Andrew said. "Do you know that one?"

"Sure. From *Strange Meeting*."

"An antiquarian pores over historical records from nineteenth-century London and tries to reconstruct the city exactly as it was. At the end he imagines another, divine antiquarian somewhere keeping track of him and his world. It makes you wonder where Horace Jacob Little would get an idea like that."

WE STOPPED FOR lunch at a diner on the outskirts of Overlook. Andrew ordered bacon and eggs. He mostly picked at the food and pushed it around the plate.

He removed a bunch of papers from his pocket and unfolded them. "I took these from Horace Jacob Little's apartment," he said. "Part of his next novel. I haven't had a chance to analyze it yet, but it seems pretty rough. Some of it's pretty nonsensical, like *Finnegans Wake*. Maybe it's a first draft."

"Would you put them away?"

After I paid the bill, I went back to the table for Andrew. He was gone. I panicked, imagining he had fled into the woods pursued by one of his illusions. The waitress told me that my brother had already gone out to the car. I found him there, playing with the radio antenna.

We rolled through Overlook's deserted downtown and seedy residential streets, and I made my way once more to the mountain above town—the overlook that the Bendersons had chosen for their magnificent house. Once again, I headed down the long driveway lined with arching elms and arrived at the Muse Asylum.

"Don't forget. Earl Jenkins. Okay?" Andrew eyed me suspiciously as he closed his door, as though I might have been about to leap into the car to return to the city.

I had called Dr. Saunders before the trip to tell him I was bringing Andrew back. He said he would "have some tea on" for us. He met us at the door with the air of a parent welcoming his children to the nest; he fretted about how tired we must have been after such a long drive, and asked how the traffic was. He shepherded us into a parlor filled with velvet-covered furniture, ornate gold-framed mirrors and dark green wallpaper highlighted with what appeared to be gold leaf. He stood at the mantelpiece, toying with an antique clock that displayed the wrong time. Soon a white-suited orderly entered the room with tea.

Taking tea seemed exactly the thing to do in that eminently civilized interior. The scene, with a few slight alterations, mostly to my clothing and Andrew's, could have taken place a century before. I wondered whether the effect was intentional—whether Dr. Saunders maintained the period-piece atmosphere to give his patients a sense of isolation not only in location, but in time as well.

"Andrew, how have you been feeling?" he asked.

"Just great, Doctor."

"Have you been taking the Rydazine?"

"Yes, I have."

I started to protest, but Dr. Saunders raised his hand to silence me. His gaze never wavered from Andrew's eyes.

"*All* the time?" he said, staring and walking toward Andrew. Although he was elderly, and trembled as he leaned on his four-toed cane, his penetrating gaze and steady, probing voice conferred authority. Andrew relented.

"Okay. Not all the time. It makes me nauseous."

"Does it? Well, I can prescribe something to counter that. What would you say to that?"

"Fine." Andrew was cowed. He looked at the Oriental rug and shrugged.

"Tell him about Horace Jacob Little," I said. Andrew turned to Dr. Saunders for permission to proceed, which was granted with a raised white eyebrow.

"You'll think it's ridiculous."

"Not at all," Dr. Saunders said. "Nothing is ridiculous. You once told me that probability includes the improbable in its outer limits."

"I have picked up some sensitive new information about him. That's all I can say now."

"We'll have plenty of time to discuss this. I'm eager to hear what you've found."

"I'll bet you are."

"Why don't you go upstairs to your old room? We've kept it the way you left it. Stay a few days. We'll adjust your dosages. We'll have you straightened out in no time."

Andrew turned to me and whispered, "What about—"

"Okay, okay," I said. "Is there a patient here named Earl Jenkins?"

"Yes. A longtime resident."

"Andrew wants me to visit him. I don't know why."

"No hints," Andrew said. "You'll see."

Dr. Saunders smiled and stared at Andrew, as though reappraising his unpredictable patient.

When we exited the room, Dr. Saunders caught my elbow and whispered, "Thank you so much for helping Andrew. He really has no one to look out for him. You've done a wonderful thing."

"He was my classmate," I said awkwardly, not knowing quite how to account for my interest in Andrew's welfare.

"You'll stay the night, won't you? It's too late to drive all the way back to New York. We have a room on the third floor that we use for guests. Perfectly isolated from the patients, of course."

AFTER REINSTALLING ANDREW in his austere room, Dr. Saunders led me up another flight of stairs, this one narrow and dark.

The doctor lowered his voice. "Earl is a most unusual patient. He sustained a severe head injury in the Vietnam War and was left with total and persistent anterograde amnesia." He raised his eyebrows as if I should be impressed by this.

"Meaning?"

"He can't form new memories. The shrapnel seems to have lesioned the hippocampus bilaterally. That alone isn't why he's here, though. It's what he does to compensate for his amnesia."

Dr. Saunders was enjoying the presentation, building suspense. I thought of the pride a mad scientist might have when showing his prize creation.

"What does he do?" I asked.

"You'll see." He raised his voice as he opened the door. "Earl, you have a visitor."

"I don't like visitors," Earl said softly.

"I know. But take a break for a few minutes. It won't be long at all."

Earl Jenkins was a thin man with delicate features and a wild shock of white hair. His cheek was marred by a shiny patch of scar tissue, like a birthmark. He was seated at a desk, surrounded by piles of paper and several volumes of what looked like ancient texts, bound in brown leather and oversized like illuminated manuscripts.

"Who are you?" he asked, without looking up from his writing.

"My name is Jake Burnett. I just came by to chat."

"I'm busy. Can't you see I'm in the middle of my city?"

Where had I seen him before? Why did everything seem familiar?

"What is your city?"

He put down his pen, and hastily opened a binder. "I'm keeping track of what everyone in London did on December 4, 1881. Itineraries, interactions, crossed paths. I do this for everyone in the city. I write it down because I can't remember things very well."

I leaped to my feet. Earl Jenkins was the antiquarian from "The History of London."

"Have you ever heard of Horace Jacob Little?" I was confused but exhilarated.

"No," he said, returning to his work. I expected some elaboration, but Earl Jenkins seemed intent on ignoring me.

"Mr. Jenkins?"

"Who are you?" he asked, in apparent sincerity, having already forgotten me.

I LEFT DR. SAUNDERS on the third floor and raced downstairs to Andrew's room. He was sitting on his bed.

"What the hell's going on?" I asked.

"'The History of London,' right?"

"He was here, wasn't he?"

Andrew stood, beaming. "Come with me. I want to show you something."

He took me to the top of the main staircase and pointed at the wall, on which hung a series of framed black-and-white photographs. In each of them, about two dozen people were gathered in the hospital's garden.

"They're the annual group photos of Overlook residents. Look at the one from 1985," he said.

I descended a few stairs and examined the picture. There was Dr. Saunders, younger but still leaning on his four-toed cane. I ran my eyes over the rest of the faces. I did not recognize any—but there was something familiar about one on the far right. I returned to the face and studied it.

"Holy shit," I said.

Andrew hit me on the arm. "You see? I told you I had a great story for you."

I could not remove my eyes from the picture. I repeated the obscenity because I couldn't think of anything else to say or do. The beard was closer-cropped and the face younger, but there was no doubt I was looking at a picture of Horace Jacob Little.

"BURNETT, WHERE THE hell are you?" Fogerty asked when I called him from a pay phone on the first floor.

"I'm back up here at Overlook."

"You missed your deadline on the city council story. We had to scramble to fill the hole. What the fuck are you doing up there?"

"I have a new lead on a follow-up to the Horace Jacob Little story. You won't believe this, but—"

"I don't care. We've wasted enough time on him. You get back here by tomorrow or you're fired. If I can't depend on you to come through by deadline, I can do without you."

I hadn't anticipated he would be so angry. I thought briefly about climbing into the car and driving all night to get back to the city, but I couldn't stand the thought of leaving the story unresolved. I would stay at the Muse Asylum. I had a few questions to ask Dr. Saunders.

chapter twenty

I had my first full dose of the Muse Asylum at dinner that night. The entire community—patients, orderlies, Dr. Saunders and the rest of his staff—ate in a single dining room. Andrew took a seat at one of the tables and motioned me over.

"I'd like you all to meet a friend of mine," he said to his table-mates. "Jake Burnett, this is Margot Edmundson, Walter Neil and Aaron Rosenblatt."

"What do you do?" Margot asked me. She was a waif of a woman, wearing turquoise earrings and a necklace with a hexagonal crystal.

"Until recently I was a reporter."

The residents looked at one another. "I don't think we've ever had a reporter here," Walter Neil said in a Texas accent. "I guess Saunders is expanding his definition of art."

"I'm not a new patient," I said. "I brought Andrew back up here."

Aaron Rosenblatt, the other person at the table, had not yet touched his food. He was humming to himself, his mind apparently elsewhere. "What do you think of this?" he asked me, then resumed his humming.

"Very good," I replied, although I couldn't really judge it since he was humming so quickly.

"My twelfth symphony. The world has never heard its like."

Meanwhile, Margot Edmundson had turned her attention to her plate. She was absorbed in the task of arranging her carrots in parallel rows.

"What do you mean, you were a reporter until recently?" Andrew said.

"I probably won't be working at the *Ledger* anymore."

Dr. Saunders had saved a place for me at his private table, and I excused myself to join him. He was the headmaster of a school full of lunatics.

"Quite a group, aren't they?" He dipped a shrimp into a bath of blood-red cocktail sauce. The main course, I had seen on the blackboard outside, involved braised leg of lamb.

"Is the food here always this good?"

"We believe that a civilized dinner is conducive to recovery. You may have noticed that we require the patients to dress for dinner."

"All this is paid for by the state?"

"Oh no, this is Benderson money. We were founded when Abraham Benderson had a nervous breakdown at the turn of the century. He was an amateur landscape painter, and my grandfather was engaged by the family to treat him. William Saunders had made a name for himself with his theory that art and neuroses spring from the same subconscious source. The Bendersons always disliked this house, so they gave the place over to William Saunders and Abraham Benderson. William convinced the family that Abraham's health would be improved by gathering around him other artistically gifted psychiatric patients, and the Muse Asylum was born. Eventually the family donated it to the state, along with an endowment, with the understanding that it would continue its function. It has been in the care of a Dr. Saunders since the beginning."

"So what do you think about Andrew?"

"He'll improve if he stays here and works on his writing. Giving him more Rydazine may also help. It was a mistake to let him go, but his rapid improvement and his eagerness to visit his ex-girlfriend were such that we couldn't justify keeping him here. We're not a prison."

Dr. Saunders paused and turned his attention to his shrimp. "I read about your interview with Horace Jacob Little," he said.

"I'd actually like to speak to you about that."

Dr. Saunders put down his silverware and smiled at me. "We can meet tomorrow afternoon. I look forward to our chat."

As people finished eating, they took their dishes to a sink in the kitchen and washed them. Dr. Saunders and I did the same. I could see how the atmosphere of the Muse Asylum might indeed calm the nerves and comfort the disturbed. Every element of life there, from the food to the opulent decor to the expression of communal solidarity in washing one's own dishes, had been carefully planned to bolster the therapeutic environment. I watched Andrew talking excitedly with the other residents. To live among friends in such a spectacular house, with no cares or worries, doing nothing but creating beautiful things—I was beginning to realize what a wonderful place the Muse Asylum was.

I SPENT THE night in a room on the third floor that was, as Dr. Saunders had promised, isolated from the residents. I locked the door anyway. As I was drifting off to sleep, I heard piano music from the floor below. Aaron Rosenblatt was composing his twelfth symphony, and the halting melodies continued throughout the night, burying themselves in my dreams.

In the morning I rose early and went for a walk in the garden. I found there another figure I recalled from the *Confessions,* the autistic painter Jacques Gris.

"Bonjour," I said. He ignored me and continued to daub color on the canvas in front of him, putting more gray into a building.

I tried to pursue the conversation, but Monsieur Gris was not interested in communicating. I wondered what it was like to be him, to have a perfect memory of streets and buildings and geometry but no interest in human contact. Like everyone else at Overlook, he would make a wonderful subject for an article—a long piece, maybe a magazine article. I could spend a few days at Overlook, collecting material and doing interviews, and then send the article around. Even if no one published it, it would be good to show people as I looked for a new and better job.

THAT AFTERNOON, ANDREW took me to a favorite spot of his about a half-mile from the hospital. The ledge we stood on afforded a panoramic view of surrounding hills and the town nestled in the valley. We were far enough north that the trees had begun to change. In a clearing in the nearby woods, someone had built a chair out of flat slabs of shale.

"I wrote the final part of my autobiography sitting there." He pointed to the throne.

We stared down at cars moving silently along the road at the foot of the mountain.

"I still can't believe he was here," I said. "Tell me exactly how you figured it out."

"I spent a lot of time looking at those group pictures. When I first got here, I suspected everyone was spying on me. Then, when I heard about Earl Jenkins, I knew Horace Jacob Little had to be involved somehow. I thought this place was a training camp for his operation, and that all the people in those pictures were alumni. I tried to memorize their faces so I would be able to identify them as agents in the future."

Andrew took a seat in the stone chair. He leaned his head back and looked up at the sky.

"When I left here before, I felt perfectly normal. The Rydazine was like a wonder drug. I didn't have any new thoughts about Horace Jacob Little. But I was still curious about him. After thinking about him for so long, I just wanted to see what he was really like. You had interviewed him, so I swiped the address, which I'm sorry about, by the way, and I went to see him."

"That's when you recognized him from the picture."

"Lara thought I was having a relapse, but I wasn't. I really did recognize him. Then I guess the Rydazine stopped working and things went downhill."

"How are you feeling now?"

"Back to normal."

I hoped the drug would continue to work its magic. The transformation was remarkable. The previous day Andrew had sat beside me during the drive up and spoken wildly about Josef Mengele. Now he sat in the makeshift chair, calm and serene, willing to accept it as nothing more than a bemusing coincidence that Horace Jacob Little had once spent time at the Muse Asylum.

"I've decided to write an article about this place," I told him. "I can't go wrong with all the unique people around here. And I can reveal that Horace Jacob Little was a patient here."

"Sounds good," Andrew said, and began to walk back toward the house.

IN THE EVENING, Dr. Saunders took me down the main corridor to show me paintings done by the residents. Some were violent compositions, with paint hurled and splattered in apparent fury. Others were murky affairs with indistinct human forms and pieces of shattered objects. One picture, by Margot Edmundson, depicted a figure surrounded and obscured by a thick fog. It was entitled *Orpheus.*

Dr. Saunders led me into his office, where red embers were glowing in the fireplace.

"Were you able to determine the purpose of your visit with Earl Jenkins?" He grunted as he kneeled to tend to the fire, which soon filled the dark room with warm and shifting illumination.

"I think it relates to one of Andrew's theories."

"A strange case, Earl Jenkins." The doctor walked unsteadily toward the chair behind his desk and settled himself carefully. "Memory for him is essentially a slippery medium. I've always been fascinated by his compulsion to counteract his deficit by trying to remember a whole city, an entire civilization."

"It reminds me of that story by Horace Jacob Little," I said.

The fire crackled and flickered lowly, casting fleeting shadows around the room and giving Dr. Saunders's bearded face a dignity that was invisible by daylight. Outside, bushes and trees were waving slowly in anticipation of a storm. There was nothing recognizably modern in the room, only those busts of Roman poets and old books, and the flames fighting the dark as in a medieval monastery. There was intimacy even in the silence, and I felt sure that my next line of questioning would be successful. There could be no secrets or mistakes within the compass of that confidential firelight.

"Horace Jacob Little says hello," I said.

Dr. Saunders smiled slyly, chuckled softly. "I was wondering whether you knew. He hasn't come by in years, but he visited many times in the past."

"He was a patient here?"

"Is that what he told you?"

"He was a little vague."

"No, he came here to do research several times before he published *Strange Meeting*. He had grown interested in the connections between madness and art. What better place to study that than the Muse Asylum?"

"And Earl Jenkins became the antiquarian in 'The History of London'?"

"Precisely."

I let out an exhalation of relief. The unexplained connection had been made clear, the loose ends tied up into one neat and logical package.

"I've decided to write an article about this place after all," I said.

"I suppose you would like me to go on the record as confirming Horace Jacob Little's interest in our community?"

"It would make an unforgettable story."

"Let me think about it."

ON MY WAY upstairs I poked my head into Andrew's room. He was standing in the dark and staring out the window, watching the wind pick up as the storm grew closer.

"I just called Lara," he said.

I sat on the edge of his bed. "What did she say?"

"We always wanted to move to California. After she finished law school, we would go out to the Sonoma Valley. That's my idea of paradise, vineyards stretching out on the hills under the soft sun. She would be a lawyer and I would do something, I never knew what. Teacher, housepainter, whatever. It didn't matter as long as I would be with her. I wanted us to live in a white house and have two kids."

"The American dream."

"When I was here last time, all I could think about was getting better and leaving to go find her. And it happened. Everything was working out. All I had to do was keep myself together, but I couldn't. I blew it."

"It's not your fault," I said. "You needed more medicine."

"She thinks it's my fault."

He had not looked at me since I entered the room. He kept staring out into the night.

"What did she say when you called?" I asked again.

"She told me not to call her. She hung up on me."

I stood and walked closer to Andrew, and placed myself just behind him. "She doesn't understand."

He turned and glared at me. "She *does* understand. She understands perfectly. If I'm lucky, I'll spend the rest of my life alternating between sanity and confusion. If I'm not, the drugs will stop working and I'll never recover. How can I expect her to stay with me? Even if she wanted to, I couldn't put her through all that."

I had no idea what to say. He was right, of course.

"I don't want to stay here." He moved toward his bed and lay down. "I want to get a bunch of medicine and go somewhere new. I'll start a new life and wait for the drugs to stop working."

"Who says they'll stop working?"

He wasn't listening. I should have told him what a privilege it was for me to know him, how he had changed the way I looked at the world. I should have told him that everything would be all right. But Andrew was wandering from thought to thought, conjuring visions of an unknown future. I said good night. He did not hear me.

I WENT UPSTAIRS, locked my door and climbed into bed. The storm outside had increased in intensity, and the wind whistled against the windowpanes. Rain drummed on the roof. Occasional thunder rumbled in the distance. From below, Aaron Rosenblatt was playing crashing chords on the piano, as if in accompaniment to the wild night. I closed my eyes and tried to sleep, but I could only listen to the wind and the thunder and the rain and the chords. Slowly, I drifted off to sleep.

I awoke later to a tremendous crack of thunder directly above me, so loud it was difficult to believe it had been made by the thin air. I heard a car alarm wail in the parking lot. Cursing the rental company for selecting such sensitive devices, I threw on some clothes and went downstairs with the key. From the front door of the building, I pointed the remote control at the car and pushed the button. The car squawked and fell silent. Before closing the door I watched the rain lashing the pavement and the trees waving wildly in the distance.

I knew I would not be able to get back to sleep. I had broken through the threshold of the night, beyond which sleep would not come—only a rapid stream of thoughts and disconnected suppositions. The storm would keep me tossing and turning.

I made my way down the dark hallway of the second floor, feeling with my hands for the door to Andrew's room. I knocked softly and opened the door a crack. I spoke his name, to no reply. His bed was disordered, the sheets and blankets twisted into a ball and resting on the bare mattress. A puddle of rainwater had collected under the window, which had apparently been open all night.

I was worried as I walked hastily down the hall to consult with Lou, the orderly on duty. Surely there was an explanation for the disorder, the water, the absence. But Lou only looked mildly surprised when I asked him where Andrew was.

"In his room, Mr. Burnett."

"No, he's not. I just looked there."

We both ran down the hall, with me in the lead.

Lou looked under the bed and found something in the tangled sheets that I had missed: a sealed envelope addressed to Lara.

"My God," I said. "I think I know where he is."

Lou and I raised the alarm and ran outside with flashlights. The rain was fierce, drops stinging my face like tiny hailstones. Within seconds our clothes were soaked through, and the cold wind whipped around us. The first sign of the trail to the overlook was a worn stretch of grass that had been transformed into a runnel by the storm. At the edge of the woods the trail widened slightly as it pushed into the darkness of the forest. The beams of our flashlights danced through the trees. We went forward, periodically calling Andrew's name into the unresponsive forest.

I reached the overlook first. Andrew was lying in the mud next to the stone chair. In one hand he clasped the wet remains of a copy of *Strange Meeting,* and near the other hand, which was open and extended as though reaching for some ephemeral conclusion, was a gun with the insignia of a buffalo on the stock.

CHAPTER TWENTY-ONE

FROM THE *CONFESSIONS* OF ANDREW WALLACE

The human circadian cycle—the body's internal clock—is slightly longer than twenty-four hours. The rhythm must be reset each day. When people are placed in darkness for prolonged periods of time, their cycles remain unadjusted and they slowly drift out of sync with the rest of the world.

This happened to me at the Muse Asylum. My nights became feverish bouts of inspiration and painful memories as I struggled to move my soul from wherever it usually resides onto blank sheets of paper. As morning approached, I translated the writings into a coded alphabet and destroyed the originals. I did this because if Horace Jacob Little was somehow to get his hands on the uncoded documents, my last defenses would be obliterated. He would have my past as well as my present and future.

I slept only a few hours a night. It seemed a great waste to abandon my soul to unconsciousness when I had finally been presented with the chance to tell my story. During the day I would wander the grounds of the hospital. There was an extensive formal garden next to the mansion that included rosebushes descended from one planted by the Empress Josephine, and flowers and trees taken from Monticello and Mount Vernon.

On one of my first days at Overlook, I saw an elderly man painting in the garden. When I approached from behind I was surprised to see he was not depicting the lilies that stood before him. He was painting a streetscape, with a narrow medieval lane opening in the distance to a view of a gray river.

—Beautiful, I said.

The man continued painting without acknowledging my presence. I understood that he wanted solitude, and I moved on. It was only later, when I came to know other residents, that I was told his name. He was known as Jacques Gris. He had come to America soon after the Second World War. He failed to respond to me not because he was waiting for an address *en français*, but because he was autistic.

Dr. Saunders showed me other works by Jacques Gris, who could paint, from memory, scenes of mid-century Paris down to the most minute detail. Dr. Saunders had gone to Paris on vacation one year and taken photographs of the scenes. When compared with Dr. Saunders's photos, the paintings are so accurate that it is clear a miracle had taken place in the brain of Jacques Gris. Drainpipes, gables, windows, streetlights are all in exactly their proper locations.

There are, however, no people in the paintings of Jacques Gris.

—To see the world in that much detail is like knowing the mind of God, said Overlook's schizophrenic playwright, Walter Neil, one night at dinner.

All the residents ate dinner together every night under a sparkling chandelier in the main dining room. I usually sat with Walter, who sometimes spent the meal in brooding silence and other times talked endlessly about whatever crossed his mind. He had been at Overlook for eight years.

He told me:

—What I've learned here is that my illness can be an asset, if I can control it and put it to good use. What I mean is, as a playwright, I try to create voices. I've been given an ear for voices. I hear in them things that are not said. Sometimes I hear voices other people don't hear. Saunders says I have to discipline the voices and put them to work for me.

Also at our table was Margot Edmundson, who had been diagnosed as obsessive-compulsive. She was a painter, and worked on each of her canvases for an average of a year. Here again, Dr. Saunders had seen in her illness an opportunity for a different sort of art.

—What kind of artist has the patience to work that long and with that much attention to detail? he asked me during one of our sessions.

Margot built her paintings in layers. Each layer had to be perfect, even if it was destined to be painted over by more layers of attempted perfection. She reminded me of the medieval stonecarvers who would not cut corners even if a sculpture was destined for the roof of a cathedral, never to be glimpsed by human eyes.

The final member of the table was Aaron Rosenblatt, a manic-depressive composer. When he was in a manic phase, snatches of piano music would echo late at night through the dark halls of Overlook. Aaron would come to the table and sing to us what he had created, practically bounding out of his chair with excitement. A few days later he would speak quietly of his conviction that he would never again successfully compose anything. A few days later, he would be back to normal, on an even keel and talking about the fate of the New York Yankees.

These were some of the people I met at the Muse Asylum.

202 ÷ DAVID CZUCHLEWSKI

—————

EVERY OTHER DAY I talked with Dr. Saunders in his office. I never felt that these visits were between doctor and patient. He would fix me tea and we would chat about my past, my writing, the other residents, world literature, psychology. He understood me, and I could tell he reserved judgment about me, just as he did for the other residents. His aim was not necessarily to cure us and send us back into society. He saw his job as similar to that of curator, or director of a think tank. He wanted to understand us, and help us understand ourselves. He wanted us to create beautiful things.

—You've suffered enough, he would tell me. Your time here is your reward for all the difficulties you've had.

Dr. Saunders liked to hear about my past, and in particular about Horace Jacob Little. Of course, it was possible he was working for Horace Jacob Little and every tidbit of information I spilled was sopped up by a clandestine listening device for the author's later consideration.

Dr. Saunders also asked about my writing. At first I was reluctant to decode my autobiography for him. He told me I might be able to publish my *Confessions* if I allowed him to advise me. Such a course of action would enable me to simultaneously demonstrate the depth of my love to Lara and expose the duplicity of Horace Jacob Little to the world.

After months of writing and revising, I began the translation. An amazing thing happened as I decoded and copied the words. All the events I had written about, even the war with Horace Jacob Little, began to seem distant. Everything had occurred out in the real world, not within the sanctuary of Overlook. For the first time in years I felt secure and invulnerable. Horace Jacob Little could not touch me while I was a resident.

I NOW THINK about Horace Jacob Little much less than I once did. I can even imagine a time when I will not need to think of him at all.

I SENSE I am coming to the end of the *Confessions*. There is a certain attraction in leaving matters unresolved. Maybe I will never leave the Muse Asylum. Maybe I will find Horace Jacob Little. Maybe he will find me. Or maybe what is to come is too strange, too chaotic and non-linear, to allow even such rudimentary conjectures based on the past. Regardless, there will be a future of some sort for me, and I will discover it alone.

I have made my statement.

This is my account of what I have done on earth and the condition of the place as I found it.

I sit below the hospital on the mountain overlooking the town. I am watching the sun decline toward the horizon, as it has done since the world was a newborn stone, devoid of atmosphere and sea. In the face of this timeless ritual, my own problems fade for a few seconds— as a flame flickers and almost goes out, but then roars back stronger than ever. So it is with my thoughts of Lara. They leave for a moment and then return, more aching, more desperate. Even if nothing else comes from all these words, I hope Lara reads them and knows they were a song to her.

Always looking in from the outside.

The sun has sunk below the mountains across the valley. The lights of Overlook have begun to twinkle like an earthbound constellation. In the last embers of the day, I arrive at the final words of my story. The words of departure, and return.

cнaртer twenty-two

I did not move the gun before the police arrived. It was a straight-forward case of suicide, but I had seen enough TV crime dramas to fear the appearance of impropriety. Instead, I bent close to the ground to examine the weapon, which was illuminated by my flash-light, and was the only visible object in a void of darkness and rain. It was definitely Horace Jacob Little's gun. Andrew must have swiped it along with the manuscript pages when he broke into the author's apartment. After worrying his whole life that Horace Jacob Little would kill him, he had done it himself, using his enemy's weapon.

I walked to the cliff, thinking of Andrew's last words to me. He had spoken of beginning a new life. How could I not have guessed what he meant? My first coherent emotion was anger. I blamed myself for not recognizing his state of mind for what it was, for not reporting the situation to Dr. Saunders. I also blamed him for giving up. There were still new drugs to try, and new chances with Lara. The cage around his soul had been weakening slowly. There was no need for this instantaneous escape.

Scenes from Andrew's life, glimpsed in his *Confessions,* raced through my mind. I had known him only a few months, and yet I carried with me inklings of the events that had once held prominence in his own thoughts. His *Confessions* was like the small space probe carrying a copy of Leonardo's drawing of man that will persist in the lonely universe after the death of the world.

Below me the town of Overlook slept. Only a few streetlights and porch lights interrupted the darkness. Two red beacons blinked atop the Benderson smokestack. Lou stood behind me, aiming his flashlight at Andrew and staring wide-eyed at the tableau.

"One of us should go back to the hospital," I said.

He nodded and set off down the trail. I stood alone with the body. It did not look like Andrew. He had died alone in driving rain and wind, and he looked the worse for it—pale blue and covered in mud. It seemed he had already started to return to the earth. Although the bullet had entered above the left temple, all that was amiss around the entrance wound was disordered hair and a trickle of blood following the curvature of the ear. I was scared to look for the exit wound.

I kneeled next to him in the mud and touched his copy of *Strange Meeting.* His hand was as cold as a rock. Here was the book I had given to Lara in Greenwich, just before we slept together for the first time. Here was the book she had given to Andrew to read before their first date. Here was the book that had triggered his descent into the unexplored fathoms of life. I had the strange sensation, itself worthy of a Horace Jacob Little story, that our fates were not only bound up with that book, but also spelled out in its pages. Andrew held it in his hand as if he had wanted to take it with him into the next world.

Loud voices came from the trail, competing with the wind. A half-dozen flashlight beams careened into the clearing. I stood behind the body, too shocked and disgusted to do anything but keep silent guard over it.

I REMEMBER ONLY vaguely my interview with the police that night. No, I said, I hadn't noticed a gun in Andrew's bag. I had not had any reason to look through it. They asked me whether I knew where he had gotten the gun. I thought briefly of explaining, but then realized my story would have struck the detectives as madness. I said I had no idea where the gun came from.

I also kept silent about the letter I had found in Andrew's room. He had written Lara's name on the back, and I wanted to honor the final request implicit in that. Anyway, the police didn't need to see the note to declare Andrew's death a suicide.

Dr. Saunders invited me to stay at the Muse Asylum until arrangements were made for the burial. I decided instead to drive back to New York. I didn't want to stay there among the mad and the dead. Dr. Saunders mentioned that Andrew's mother would fly in from Phoenix.

"Andrew's mother," I said. "I never really thought of him as having parents."

"He shut them out of his life. His father died while he was at Princeton. Andrew didn't go to the funeral. His mother kept track of him, though. She even had private detectives follow him to see how he was doing. In fact, she was the one who called me when Andrew was arrested. She got him into Overlook."

"She hired people to follow her son, who was paranoid about people following him?"

"It would appear so."

It was not my place to question his mother's strategies for keeping tabs on her estranged son, but I wondered how many of Horace Jacob Little's "agents" were truly figments of Andrew's imagination.

I CALLED LARA to tell her that Andrew was dead. Aside from a long pause after I finished the story, there was no discernible reaction. Lara was not the type to go in for public wailing. I assumed she would deal with the finality of the news when she was alone in the room with the dial tone.

I told her the memorial service was scheduled for early morning two days later.

"I'm driving up tomorrow afternoon," I said. "Do you want a ride?"

"You're staying there the night before the funeral?"

"We can stay at the hospital. You can have the guest room and I'll sleep on a couch."

"I have a class I can't miss tomorrow evening. I'll drive up after."

I was struck by the seriousness and terseness of her tone. It was as if we were conducting a tough business negotiation.

"I'm sorry," I said.

"I know," she replied, and hung up.

I DECIDED GEORGE should also know what had happened.

"Poor guy," he said. "Lara must be at the end of her rope."

"I guess so. We didn't have a very long conversation."

"Still, she must be relieved it's over."

I hoped this wasn't true, but I knew a part of Lara must have felt released from a burden.

"The funeral is the day after tomorrow," I said. "In case you can make it."

"I'm really swamped here. Besides, I didn't really know him."

There was no logical basis for my expecting George to go to Andrew's funeral, but his resistance to the idea annoyed me. I wanted as many people as possible at the service. To have only a few mourners standing around his grave seemed to me a condemnation of his life—perhaps a just verdict, but a condemnation nonetheless.

"Give me the address," George said. "I'll send some flowers."

EARLY THE NEXT morning I took the subway to Columbia. I asked around until I found the Department of Comparative Literature, where a secretary pointed me in the direction of Professor Mullin's office. I found him typing away at his computer, with his back to me.

At my knock he swiveled in his chair and lowered his face to peer above his reading glasses.

"You may not remember me," I said. "I took your contemporary novel class at Princeton."

He put his hand to his temple and closed his eyes, as though trying to soothe a headache. "Don't tell me. Jake Burnett, right? What can I do for you? Are you at Columbia now?"

"No. Actually, I'm here to deliver some news. I was friends with Andrew Wallace."

Mullin, who had been pleased by his feat of memory, now turned wary. He regarded me as though I might have been about to attack him.

"He's dead," I said. " He committed suicide yesterday morning."

"Thank God."

I must have looked shocked at this reaction, because he continued: "Of course I'm sorry for him. I know he couldn't help himself. Watching this brilliant kid self-destruct while he worked on his thesis was one of the most horrible things I've ever seen. I tried to help him.

I talked to his girlfriend about what we could do for him. But then there were the letters, the death threats, the nonstop calls to my house, the thing with my car."

"I didn't know it was that bad."

"You don't have kids, do you? It's one thing to worry about your own safety, but my daughter was a different story. Every minute she was out of my sight, I had to live with the thought he might do something to her. I'm sorry for him, but this is the best news I've heard in a long while."

I wanted to argue with him, to tell him that Andrew was a good person despite all the confusion. But to Mullin he was a menace, and I'm not sure that in his shoes I would have reached a different conclusion.

He shook his head as I stood to leave.

"What a fucking waste," he said.

"One question before I go. Remember that crazy guy who interrupted your lecture claiming he was Horace Jacob Little? You suggested he might have been an actor you hired. Was he?"

Mullin smiled. "If I recall, that lecture was given on the first day of the cruelest month."

I DROVE UPSTATE lost in thought. Outside, the leaves were red, gold and orange under a gray sky. Summer had ended. The days were shortening. The earth was shutting down after a season or two of life and the world was suffused with melancholy. At least that's how I saw it. I couldn't quite pin down my feelings. I had known Andrew for only a few months, but his death was affecting me disproportionately. Something about his story had touched me, so that he was not simply a classmate, or even a friend, but a stand-in for some aspect of myself. Aside from the exaggerations and distortions inherent in his condition, we were not very different. Everything that had happened to him from senior year onward was unfair. I personally resented it, as if all along *I* had been the one trapped by life or by God in an absurd and meaning-less fantasia of paranoia. Mullin's final analysis was a perfect summary of Andrew's life. What a fucking waste.

"THIS IS SOME place," Lara said when she arrived late that night. I was reclining on a couch in the main parlor, reading *The New York Times*. She sat at the other end of the couch.

"How are you doing?" I asked.

"Fine."

Her tone was matter-of-fact, her face almost expressionless.

"Andrew mentioned you that night," I said. "He told me you wanted to move out to California together."

"Did he tell you about the cat we would have? We wanted to name it Schrödinger. Get it?"

"Help me out."

"Schrödinger came up with the thought experiment where you put a cat in a box with uranium that may or may not decay and kill it. The point is, until you check to see what happened, the cat is sus-pended in a world between life and death. We wanted to get a cat and name him after Schrödinger. That's the kind of thing Andy and I used to laugh about. A regular pair of geeks."

She ran a hand over the fabric on the arm of the sofa, letting the smile die on her face.

"My parents wouldn't come to the service," she said. "I told them it would mean a lot to me, but they didn't like Andy, even before senior year."

"Why not?"

"They didn't understand him. They were right, of course. It was crazy to think about me the way he did."

"It wasn't crazy. It was the logical extension of how he felt about you. In fact, I wish I had done the same. If I could have taken a lesson from Andrew, you and he would never have gotten together in the first place."

She saw what I meant and regarded me from the corner of her eyes. "Don't make this any more difficult than it already is."

I wondered whether I should tell her about Horace Jacob Little's sojourn at the Muse Asylum.

"I look back on how Andy and I were at Princeton and I feel like I'm looking back on childhood," she said. "The thought never crossed my mind that something like this could happen to him. I feel like an adult now, like I've seen something ugly from life."

"It wasn't ugly. Even if it didn't turn out right, there was something beautiful about Andrew's life, something uncorrupted."

"Don't you think I know how wonderful he was? He was my twin."

"What do you mean?"

"He and I once watched this program about identical twins, how they turn out the same even if they're raised apart, how one twin always knows what the other one is thinking. And we decided that we were twins, figuratively. That was how we felt together. But what's the point of getting upset? That's how things work, right? You get the rug pulled out from under you, you get up. You move on. What's the point of sitting around crying about it?"

"This is a funeral. You're allowed to cry."

She was becoming exasperated. I fingered Andrew's letter to her in my pocket.

"Why do you have this need to see me lose it?" she said. "It's like you want some proof that I loved him."

"What did you say to him the other night? When he called from here?"

"That I didn't want to talk to him. What the hell was I supposed to say? I was so mad at him. No, not at him. I was just so mad. I had no idea . . ."

She was looking up at the ceiling, shaking her head.

"He wrote this to you on the night he died." I held the envelope out for her. She stood and took a step away from me.

"Take it," I said. She looked back and forth between the letter and my face.

"I can't," she said in an uncertain voice. She wiped her eye with the heel of her hand.

"You're kidding." I tried to put the letter in her hand.

"No," she said fiercely, pushing my hand away.

She wasn't going to open it, and I wasn't about to throw it away. I broke the seal and unfolded the letter. Immediately she overcame her reservations and sat down beside me to read it.

"My God," she said.

It was not a letter. It was a sheet of paper covered in Andrew's writing, all the words on top of one another. He must have crowded a thousand words on that single side of the paper. After close inspection, I saw that he had written only a single word, over and over, until the white of the underlying page was obliterated.

You.

Lara grabbed the letter and crumpled it up, as if to throw it. Instead, she hugged the wadded page to her stomach and started to cry, fighting it at first and then succumbing. She sank into the couch and I put my arms around her.

"Andy," she said three times.

She sat up and wiped her eyes, looking at me. "I'm sorry," she said.

"Don't be."

I cared for her more than ever. She was no longer an object of lust or adolescent devotion, but simply a friend who was coming to understand the chance she had lost. I had a faint intimation of what she must have felt, based on my own confusion and darkness when I lost her. But that was in the past. Everything was fading into the past, until all that remained was the two of us in that silent, lonesome mansion, sitting up late in the parlor, Lara with tears shining on her handsome cheeks, and me with nothing much to say.

THE NEXT MORNING, low clouds obscured the Benderson smokestack and a general wetness hung in the air—now light rain, now a hovering mist. Lara and I went directly to the cemetery where the brief memorial service was to be held. We were the first ones there, and I was enlisted to help the cemetery crew place Andrew's coffin next to the grave site. It was not heavy.

A minibus arrived from the Muse Asylum with a dozen residents and Dr. Saunders. Mrs. Wallace pulled up in what I assumed was a rented car. The priest walked over from the nearby church.

Words were spoken, flowers dropped. The rain thickened, blowing under the small plastic tent and drumming on the coffin. I did not pay much attention to the service. I was imagining Andrew in a place where he would be free to indulge his passions. I recalled from the *Confessions* that he had asked God to let him live forever in one moment, when he saw Lara playing with the handle of her coffee mug. I am not a religious person, but I hoped he was not disappointed.

Lara and I were walking back to our cars after the service when Mrs. Wallace caught up to us.

"Are you Lara?" she asked. "It's so nice to finally meet you. Andy and I didn't talk much, but when we did he always mentioned you."

Mrs. Wallace dug through her purse and extracted a photograph. "I thought you might like to have this." She offered the photo with an outstretched hand.

It was Andrew at about age nine, staring at the shadow thrown by a stick planted upright in a field.

"Do you know what he's doing? He's measuring the circumference of the earth. He read in a magazine how the ancient Greeks did it, and he set out to do it himself. He came pretty close."

Lara laughed softly and thanked Mrs. Wallace, who nodded grimly and walked away.

"Measuring the earth with a stick," Lara said. "That is so Andy."

She touched the picture with her index finger, removing a speck of dust from little Andrew's face. She put the picture in her wallet and carefully closed it. When we reached her car, we hugged. She held on to me for a long time, longer than good-bye.

"We'll talk back in the city," I said. Lara nodded and drove away into the gray rain.

CHAPTer TWenTY-THree

As I watched Lara's car moving down the cemetery road, Dr. Saunders approached me. He was moving gingerly over the muddy turf with his cane.

"I wanted to thank you again for all you did for Andrew," he said. "You were a true friend. Before you go, come back to the hospital. I want to give you something."

I followed the minivan to the Muse Asylum. The patients piled out and were counted by Lou. I thought of children returning from a field trip.

Dr. Saunders led me into his office and closed the door. He picked up a manila envelope from his desk and handed it to me.

"I had a copy made of the group photograph with Horace Jacob Little," he said. "For your article."

"I doubt I'm going to write it. I kind of want to get out of here."

He looked disappointed. "Well, I'd still like you to have this, as a token of thanks."

I opened the envelope and examined the photo. There was Horace Jacob Little—tall and broad, bearded and staring malevolently at the camera.

"Does he look the same?" Dr. Saunders asked.

"His beard is huge now," I said. "But he's as massive as ever."

"What do you mean?"

"You know. Tall and imposing."

Dr. Saunders shook his head. "Not Horace Jacob Little. Look at me right next to him—he's only as tall as I am. Or as I was."

The man standing next to Dr. Saunders didn't bear even the slightest resemblance to the person I called Horace Jacob Little. I stared at the picture for so long that Dr. Saunders asked me if something was wrong.

"*That's* Horace Jacob Little?" I asked, pointing to a short, balding man. "Him?"

"I've always thought the expression on his face captured his personality so well. A tremendously learned man—gentle, sensitive, dreamy. I'm sure he's still much the same."

"Who's that?" I tried to maintain a casual tone as I pointed at my Horace Jacob Little.

"That's one of the patients. Gabriel Callahan. He was a brilliant writer, probably the most talented person we've ever treated."

"Is he still here?"

"No, he left soon after this picture was taken. He wouldn't say where he was going, and we never heard from him again. It's a shame, really. If he had stayed, he might have become a great writer. Now who knows what's become of him?"

Was it possible that Dr. Saunders was mistaken, or perhaps senile? No. He was gazing at me steadily, clearly in full command of his faculties. With a combination of fear and euphoria, I felt myself falling, embracing a warm cushion of air. I slumped into a seat.

"Was Gabriel Callahan dangerous?"

"Why are you so interested in Gabriel?"

"He looks so fierce in the picture. He dominates everyone around him."

"Strictly speaking, none of our patients is dangerous. We don't have the necessary security measures in place. But Gabriel was given to angry outbursts and violent episodes. Between you and me, if he hadn't been such a good writer, I doubt we would have taken him."

Had Andrew had been *right* about "Strange Meeting"? This Gabriel Callahan slips away from the mental facility in the wake of Horace Jacob Little's visit, only to present himself to me, years later, as the authentic person. My heart surged, because after all of Andrew's struggles and disappointments, I felt this news had the power to redeem him.

Then I remembered my words to the person I called Horace Jacob Little. Suspecting nothing, I had told him that Andrew thought "Strange Meeting" was based on a true story. Andrew himself might have accused him of murder to his face. If this Gabriel Callahan had killed the original author, the dreamy-eyed bald man, what else would he have done to preserve his secret?

"About Andrew," I said, my voice unsteady, "did the police rule the death officially a suicide?"

"As far as I know."

"Is it possible someone else fired the gun?"

Dr. Saunders was beginning to look suspicious. "Do you know something you're not telling me?"

I paused and considered my answer. Dr. Saunders was sitting behind his desk, pulling gently on his beard. I had to tell him. It would mean a lot of unpleasantness for everyone, especially for Lara, but I had no other choice.

"The person you call Horace Jacob Little"—I pointed to the bald man—"he isn't the Horace Jacob Little I interviewed." I shifted my finger to Gabriel Callahan: "This is the person I interviewed."

Dr. Saunders looked at me as if I had lapsed unexpectedly into an incomprehensible foreign language.

"Andrew was right all along," I said. "Gabriel Callahan murdered Horace Jacob Little. He may have killed Andrew to protect his secret. In fact, the gun belonged to Gabriel Callahan. I assumed Andrew had stolen it, but now I'm not so sure."

Dr. Saunders leaned across the desk and adopted the soothing tone I had heard him use with Andrew. "Tell me more," he said.

"You don't believe me?"

"Why don't you stay here for a few days?"

He regarded me as though I had suddenly become an interesting clinical subject. I could see that his mind was already at work, perhaps formulating a journal article about the friend of a deceased mental patient who deals with his grief by adopting and furthering the obsessions of the deceased.

"I think I'll go back to the city now," I said.

He picked up his cane and waved it toward me, more in warning than in valediction. "You take care," he said. "If you ever need a place to escape from the world, remember us here."

As I sped down the highway, I spent more time peering into my rearview mirror than I did keeping track of the road ahead. I slowed to forty, then sped up to ninety, to see whether anyone would stick with me. I had inadvertently revealed to Gabriel Callahan that

Andrew had discovered his true identity. He might assume I would be a similar threat, to be dealt with in a similar manner.

MY FIRST ACTION on reaching my apartment was to load the Cafarellas' gun, which I had left undisturbed since my arrival. I had never handled a gun, much less shot one. I went to the roof of the apartment building to make sure I knew how to use it. I deduced which button was the safety, and once it was off I pointed the gun to the sky and pulled the trigger. The weapon sprang to life, discharging an enormous explosion and jolting my arm farther upward. Pigeons all around me made for safety, filling the air with fluttering. The noise echoed off the surrounding buildings and slowly dissipated.

I spent the next two days locked in the apartment, not venturing outside. I stayed at the window and watched the world below, trying to see whether anyone was waiting for me outside, whether anyone had been double-parked for a suspiciously long period of time. When I saw nothing out of the ordinary, I relaxed somewhat. Gabriel Callahan, after all, had no real evidence that I knew his secret. As long as I didn't find him and accuse him, he would assume that Andrew had kept the truth to himself, or that I hadn't believed him. Gabriel Callahan had probably moved away to a safer locale, where his identity would be less likely in question.

To check this theory, I went to Central Park West and observed Horace Jacob Little's building from my old post in the park. I brought the gun for self-defense, and I was more than ready to use it. The apartment windows were dark both night and day, however, and I never saw him enter or exit the building.

I made a few phone calls to real estate brokers until I found someone who was able to confirm that the apartment was empty. A perky woman named Janet told me that, yes, 4-A was in fact for rent.

She quoted the monthly payment and broker's fee, and we made an appointment to meet there the next afternoon.

I was in no position to rent the place, and I felt guilty about wasting the poor woman's day, but I wanted to go up there one last time.

THE APARTMENT WAS indeed empty, but the ghost of Horace Jacob Little floated with the dust stirred up by the removal of the furniture and books. Janet prattled on about the kitchen and the sizable bathroom and the quality of the hardwood floors. My mind was elsewhere. I remembered conducting an interview in that very place in the vain hope that my interlocutor would let fall a pearl of his apparently boundless wisdom. It was there that he had brandished the gun, soon to discharge a bullet in a hidden moment in the dark woods of Overlook.

I kept imagining those final moments—Andrew running down the path to the overlook, whipped by the branches and the rain, Gabriel Callahan behind him, with quivering lips, intent on preserving his secret. Had Andrew found some satisfaction in the fact that his lifelong fear of Horace Jacob Little had proved justified? Or was he only frightened and lonely? He must have thought of Lara in the last seconds, as Gabriel Callahan raised that gun to his temple. Andrew must have submitted to this fate without a fight; the police had found no sign of struggle. I had called Dr. Saunders a few times to ask for details about their report—powder residue, powder burns, the distance from which the bullet had been fired. He would say only, "Everything's in order. I know you find it hard to accept—we all do—but Andrew killed himself that night."

Dr. Saunders was old friends with Horace Jacob Little *and* Gabriel Callahan's former doctor. Where did his loyalties lie? Whom was he protecting?

I wandered from room to room, thinking that Gabriel Callahan had perhaps left something behind. Was it unreasonable to expect a coded message of some sort? That's what Andrew would have looked for—a pattern in the dust or a line scratched on the window that would have become the central text of a wild adventure, even if it meant nothing to the rest of us. I found myself wishing for his openness to possibility.

Janet was surprised when I looked behind the radiator, inside the medicine cabinet, on top of shelves in the kitchen. I told her I wanted to check out every inch of the place. I thought I saw her roll her eyes.

After several minutes of this madness, I passed the phone in the kitchen. Janet was in the living room, riffling through some papers in the misguided hope that I would sign something.

I pressed the Redial button.

A woman answered: "Leslie Greene."

"Is Gustave there?" I asked.

"There's no one here by that name."

"This isn't Aerotech, Inc.?"

The woman laughed. "We're a literary agency."

"What number is this?"

She gave a number. I scribbled it in my reporter's notebook, which I carried out of habit. I told her I had transposed the seven and the nine, and hung up.

I thanked Janet and said I would keep the place in mind. I left amid a flurry of business cards and talk of certified checks and deposits.

GABRIEL CALLAHAN HAD become invisible. In any town, in any city, on any continent, a tall man could show up from parts unknown, probably shorn of his beard. He would rent a room, keep to himself, write the stories that held the world and a dead man's name captive. And if anyone should get too close to him, to the dirty mechanics of the creative process, "Horace Jacob Little" would rear up and strike him down.

As I sat lost in thought on the subway, something flew into my face. I winced and waved my hands convulsively. It felt like a huge roach made airborne.

When the object had become disengaged from my hair, I followed my fellow travelers' gazes toward the ceiling, where a spectacular butterfly was flitting among the fluorescent lights and air-conditioning vents, regal blue and gold and green against the pale beige of the grimy car. Around me, people smiled and followed the butterfly's erratic path with rapt attention. Where did that come from, they seemed to be thinking. A butterfly down here!

It must have flown into the train as it sat in the staging yard, only to be carried along into the rushing underground. I was filled with anxiety. I felt the butterfly's plight as if it were my own—plucked from the midst of my life, trapped underground and transported in a strange conveyance to an unceremonious death. I imagined the creature finding an open window and escaping into the tunnel, never again to see daylight, buffeted by the roaring approach of never-ending subway trains, frustrated in its attempts to soar away from its incomprehensible difficulties.

I stood and followed the butterfly down the car with cupped hands. People saw my intention and made room. I leaped and lunged, climbed on seats, stalked slowly when it was at rest. And finally I closed the cage of my hands around it and felt its wings beating in a frenzy of fear.

I returned to my seat, waving with the motion of the subway, and parted my hands slightly at the thumbs, then placed them before my eyes. I peered inside and saw the intricate scales of color on the wings, gold, green and blue, affixed in small flakes that resembled individual brush tips loaded with bright wet oil paint. And the labyrinth of the complex eye, reflecting my world in a thousand subtly different versions, the antennae waving in search of signals meaningless to me, the proboscis rolled like a tiny fire-hose. The butterfly sat immobile in my hands, as though watching me, or waiting. I was transfixed, and at the same time puzzled that something could be so beautiful that I almost wanted it to die so that others, perhaps in a distant museum, could see it as I had. I clapped my thumbs back together, rose and exited at the next station.

Once outside, I opened my hands and the butterfly took to the air, soaring into the sky and rising in compensation for the hours spent in exile under the earth.

I looked around and was surprised to find myself not far from the Brooklyn Heights promenade, where I had met Lara to fill her in on Andrew's condition. I decided to go there and watch the approaching sunset.

When I reached the promenade and stood before the Manhattan skyline, I again felt anonymous in the sweep and silence of that human constellation. I meditated on the beauty of the butterfly and my silent joy at freeing it. So much time had passed since I had felt an innocent wonder at the world, at the patchwork of figures and objects and symbols that attend our every moment. Andrew had felt that wonder, and I longed for his eyes, his voice.

I contemplated my next move. I wanted to vindicate Andrew— not by killing Gabriel Callahan, whom I doubted I could find, but by telling people what had happened. When I tried this with Dr. Saunders he thought I was losing my mind. But if I could tell the story precisely as it had taken place, then surely it would be believable.

I removed the notebook from my coat pocket and stared at the number for Leslie Greene, who must have been Horace Jacob Little's literary agent. And then an idea occurred to me.

I looked into the darkening sky, searching for the source of the unexpected revelation. I would send an account of what I had witnessed to Leslie Greene as if it were in fact written by Horace Jacob Little. She would regard it as sly postmodern playfulness, this device of the author's including himself in the plot of his novel. She would assume that Horace Jacob Little had invented the narrator Jake Burnett.

If Gabriel Callahan had convinced everyone that he was Horace Jacob Little, then why couldn't I do the same? I would write more under Horace Jacob Little's name. I would go into hiding, perhaps accompanied by Lara, and Gabriel Callahan would have to find *me*, across years, cities, countries, continents. I would be ready for him.

And if Leslie Greene discovered the ruse, I would simply publish the book under a different pseudonym—something long and intricate, perhaps Slavic or Russian. I turned and gazed at my forlorn companions, the sad misfits who were there to drink alcohol from paper bags and pass the night. *I will include you,* I thought with a rush of childish euphoria, *even you!*

I took out a pen and flipped through my notebook. Quotations filled most of the pages, fragments of the interviews I had conducted over the past few weeks, as well as some notes I had made at the Muse Asylum.

There, where the clean open page met those scribbles, I began to write. Behind me night was falling. Gray light had settled on the retreating world, the factories, the houses, the highways, the tenements, the churches, the parklands, the boardwalks, the side streets. And lost somewhere in that vastness was Horace Jacob Little, my nemesis, my identity, a spirit merged once more with the humanity from which he arose.

Thanks to Joyce Carol Oates, my teacher and advisor, for her guidance and encouragement. Thanks also to Faith Sale, for favoring me with her confidence; to Aimee Taub, a magnificent editor; to Elly Sidel, my agent; and to my family, friends, and teachers, who inspired me to write this story in the first place.